Hacking Timbuktu

A NOVEL BY STEPHEN DAVIES

 CLARION BOOKS | HOUGHTON MIFFLIN HARCOURT | BOSTON   NEW YORK | 2010

FOR KEITH AND LYNNE

Clarion Books
215 Park Avenue South, New York, New York 10003
Copyright © 2009 by Stephen Davies
First American edition 2010
Originally published in the United Kingdom in 2009 by Andersen Press Limited

The text was set in 12.5-point Fournier.
Title hand lettering by Leah Palmer Preiss
Map by Kayley LeFaiver
Book design by Sharismar Rodriguez

Clarion Books is an imprint of Houghton Mifflin Harcourt Publishing Company.

www.hmhbooks.com

Library of Congress Cataloging-in-Publication Data
Davies, Stephen, 1976–
Hacking Timbuktu / by Stephen Davies.
p. cm.
Summary: London sixteen-year-old Danny Temple and friend Omar use their computer
and parkour skills to elude pursuers as they follow clues in an Arabic manuscript to the
mysterious cliffs of Bandiagara in sub-Saharan Africa seeking an ancient treasure.

ISBN 978-0-547-39016-1

[1. Adventure and adventurers—Fiction. 2. Buried treasure—Fiction. 3. Parkour—
Fiction. 4. Computer hackers—Fiction. 5. Tombouctou (Mali)—Fiction. 6. Mali—
Fiction.] I. Title.

PZ7.D2845Hac 2010   [Fic—dc22]

Manufactured in the United States of America
DOC 10 9 8 7 6 5 4 3 2 1
4500253560

ACKNOWLEDGMENTS

A big thank-you to urban monkey Joe Morriss for
reading the parkour bits and making suggestions,
and to Kybernetikos for his amazing insights
into the world of hacking.

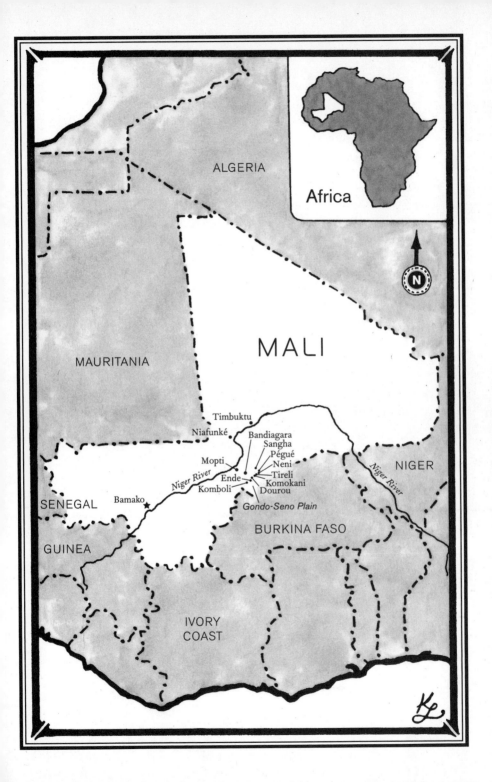

Blind and silent as a mole, Akonio Dolo crawled toward the gold. It was a tight squeeze, but Akonio didn't mind. He loved his tunnel. He had enjoyed planning it, he had enjoyed digging it, and most of all he had enjoyed stealing gold through it.

The silence was broken by footsteps in the mosque above. That had to be Sheikh al-Qadi, high professor of Timbuktu, arriving to sing the morning call to prayer. Akonio Dolo lay still and listened to the soft, unhurried footfalls of the sheikh.

The call to prayer began, but to Akonio's surprise the voice did not belong to Sheikh al-Qadi. It was far deeper and richer than al-Qadi's voice, and it reverberated down through the earth in a way that made the boy's spine tingle with pleasure.

"Allahu Akbar! Allahu Akbar!"

"God is great," breathed Akonio, and he wriggled forward again. *God is great.* The quality of the new caller's voice was extraordinary—pure yet powerful, a voice to get even the most

1

impious student out of bed at dawn. Not that there were many impious students in Timbuktu. Only one, according to Sheikh al-Qadi. He had always said that Dolo the Dogon would come to no good.

"Come to prayer, come to prayer.
Come to success, come to success."

"Come to success," breathed Akonio Dolo, edging ever closer toward the vault at the end of the tunnel. He knew what awaited him in that vault: a wall of pure gold two ingots thick. A year and a half ago the wall had been nine ingots thick, but Akonio had been working hard. So far he had stolen almost two million mithqals of gold, making him the second richest person in the whole of Mali at the age of only seventeen! It was a beautiful heist. So long as the wall remained intact on the guards' side, no one would realize there was a single mithqal missing.

"God is great! God is great!
There is no god but God!"

A tiny shower of earth fell from the tunnel roof onto the back of Akonio's neck. The boy thief frowned. Above him the voice of the prayer caller rumbled louder still.

"Prayer is better than sleep!
Prayer is better than sleep!"

A clump of earth fell onto the tunnel floor behind Akonio, and he glanced round in surprise. "Don't let me down, tunnel," he whispered. "These past two hundred nights I've found no fault in you. Don't waver now."

The tunnel replied by dumping a heavy shower of dirt on his head.

It's the vibrations caused by the new caller's voice, thought Akonio. *That voice is going to bury me alive!* He began to wriggle forward with a new urgency, legs kicking back and forth, fingernails scrabbling on the dirt floor.

"In the name of God the Compassionate, the Merciful," sang the caller, and a whole section of roof collapsed on Akonio's legs. He flailed desperately to free himself, and when at last his feet came loose, he crawled ahead at breakneck speed, blinking against a rain of laterite. He could not be far from the end of the tunnel. Any moment now he would feel the welcome draft of the vault.

"Guide us to the straight path, the path of those whom You have favored, not of those who have incurred Your wrath, nor of those who have gone astray."

WHUMP! The tunnel roof collapsed completely, knocking all the breath out of the boy's body. Instinctively Akonio turned his head face-down to make a tiny pocket of air under nose and mouth. He tried to arch his back against the weight on top of him, but it was no good. He was pinned from head to toe, as helpless as the butterflies that lined al-Qadi's study walls. The pocket of air would last for what—five shallow breaths? Ten at most.

The caller had stopped his recital. He must have heard the subsidence and felt the floor of the prayer room dimple and pucker beneath his feet—enough to make even the most fervent caller pause for thought.

All around Akonio Dolo the earth throbbed with the words of the Book. "Praise be to God, Lord of the Universe, the Compassionate, the Merciful, Sovereign of the Day of Judgment." With his final breaths Akonio couldn't help wondering what judgment God would pass on him. Would God agree with Sheikh al-Qadi's assessment? *I always knew that Dolo the Dogon would come to no good.*

Akonio wept. Sheikh al-Qadi disliked him only because he slept in class. But God knew all the facts—God knew how hard it was for a boy to stay awake in class after a busy night of tunneling. And God knew that the theft was not Akonio's fault. It was inevitable! What kind of fool stacked gold nine ingots thick from floor to ceiling and wall to wall in a vault dug out of *earth?* They were simply *asking* for someone to tunnel in. It would have been rude of Akonio *not* to have stolen the gold!

The boy took another feeble breath. Who was he trying to kid? He was a miserable thief. He knew it, God knew it, end of story. And at that moment he couldn't help but wonder: *If you're already buried, is it too late to repent?*

The boy thief pricked up his ears. *What was that?* The heavy clink of gold on gold, muted but unmistakable. Someone was dismantling the wall of ingots in the vault. The guards had heard the tunnel collapse and were coming to investigate.

"Look at this!" The voice was not far away from where Akonio lay. "This pile is only two ingots thick!"

"No! It should be nine."

"There's a gap where the gold should be."

"Can you get in?"

"I think so."

Akonio's heart pulsed weakly against the earth below. His air supply was exhausted. He was going to die.

"There's some kind of tunnel here! It looks like it's collapsed!"

"That explains the sound we heard."

"There's a lot of loose earth. I'll just try and—*wallaahi!!!!*"

"What is it?"

"Fingers! I've found fingers!"

"Thieving fingers, I'll be bound. Wait there, Yusuf, we'll come and help you."

Working together, the guards scrabbled to remove the body of the thief from its tomb, clearing earth from hands, arms, head, and shoulders. The youngest guard gave a sudden cry of recognition.

"It's the Dogon boy! It's Akonio Dolo!"

"I don't believe it," said another. "All this time, he's been stealing gold from right under our noses."

"Grab his armpits. Let's get him out of here."

The guards yanked the boy out of his hole and manhandled him through the wall of gold, up the steps, and out into the open air.

They laid him down by the eastern wall of the great Sankore

mosque. This mosque was the beating heart of Timbuktu University. It was built entirely of mud brick, except for one hundred fifty short cedar sticks protruding at regular intervals from the walls and minaret, sticks that served as scaffolding for the annual repairs to the flawless façade. Akonio Dolo looked very small next to the magnificent building.

The guards stood around the body, unsure of their next step.

"We should wash it and prepare it for burial," said one.

"We should cut off its hands," said another.

"That's not for us to decide," said a third. "We'll wait here for Sheikh al-Qadi."

The sheikh was already on his way. White robes billowed around him as he hurried to where the guards stood.

"It's Dolo the Dogon!" exclaimed the sheikh. "Why is he so dirty?"

"He's dead."

"Dead! How so?"

"The tunnel collapsed on top of him."

"What tunnel?"

"The tunnel he used for stealing gold."

A muscle in the sheikh's jaw twitched. "You mean he actually got some?"

"More than some. He got hundreds of ingots."

"What? Where did he put it all?"

"We don't know."

The sheikh spun round to face the rising sun and tore his outer robe from top to bottom. "Betrayed by one of our own!"

he cried. Sheikh al-Qadi was a dignified man, and the guards were surprised by this sudden display of passion.

"Quickly!" cried the sheikh. "Go and search the boy's room!"

When the guard came back, he said, "A camel saddle, a few clothes—and this." He held out a wad of paper.

"*Introduction to Magic Squares,*" read the sheikh, "by Abu al-Kabari." He riffled the pages and threw them petulantly to the ground. "It's nothing," he muttered. "An old mathematics treatise from the university library."

If only you knew, thought Akonio Dolo.

Akonio Dolo was not quite dead; at least he didn't think he was. He breathed in slowly through earth-caked nostrils and felt his lungs fill with air.

"Look!" said a voice. "Look there! Am I going mad, or do dead Dogon breathe?"

Akonio recognized the voice. It was one of the university doctors. *Don't check my pulse,* he thought. *Don't check my pulse.* He heard footsteps in the sand, felt the doctor kneel down beside him, felt two gentle fingers on his wrist. *Play dead,* he thought. *Play dead, play dead.*

"He's still alive," said the doctor.

Here goes. Akonio Dolo opened his eyes, sprang to his feet, and rent the heavens with a bloodcurdling Dogon war cry. The doctor yelped and fell over backward.

In front of Akonio stood a dozen guards, three tutors, a magistrate, and a growing crowd of students. Behind him, solid and impenetrable, loomed the east wall of the mosque.

The time for playing dead was past. The time had come to die properly. Snorting earth and blood from his nostrils, Akonio strode forward, and the crowd shrank back in alarm.

It was Sheikh al-Qadi who broke the Dogon's spell. "What are you waiting for?" he roared. *"Seize him!"*

As the guards surged forward, Akonio Dolo turned and ran full tilt toward the wall of the mosque. He leaped high, grabbed the lowest of the cedar sticks, and muscled up until he was standing on top of it. Up and up he climbed from stick to stick, faster and faster, a dazzling combination of leaps, swings, and muscle-ups.

"Look at him go!" exclaimed the magistrate.

"He's a born climber," murmured the doctor. "A true Dogon."

"Students!" cried the sheikh. "Form an inner and an outer circle all around the mosque. Quickly! Don't let him get away!"

The students scattered to obey, but all the while they kept their eyes fixed on their clambering classmate. Silhouetted against the lightening sky and flowing like water up the minaret, he seemed somehow heroic—a solitary soul on his way to heaven.

"Guards!" cried the sheikh. "Don't stand there like donkeys. Climb up and bring the Dogon down!"

Slowly, awkwardly, the guards began to pick their way up the wall in pursuit of Akonio Dolo.

The boy thief had already reached the pinnacle of the minaret. He squatted on top, rested his chin on his hand, and gazed at the sun as it climbed above the horizon. The east side of the minaret turned a glorious rose red.

"Dolo!" roared the sheikh. "What did you do with the gold?"

Akonio tore his gaze away from the rising sun and looked down at the sheikh. "I took it to Dogon country," he called. "It took me six separate journeys to shift it all!"

The sheikh raised his hands imploringly toward the minaret. "Where did you hide it, Akonio?"

"In the cliffs of Bandiagara! In a secret chamber nineteen ghalva northeast of Tireli."

Sheikh al-Qadi turned to the doctor and whispered, "Go and tell the stable boy to prepare the fastest stallion."

"You'll need the key!" shouted Akonio.

"And where is that?"

"The key can only be found by a Dogon. It takes a Dogon to know a Nommo!"

"Talk sense, boy!"

"Fine!" Akonio Dolo stood up on the pinnacle of the minaret. "How's this for sense? God is great!"

"He's going to jump!" yelled the doctor, starting forward.

Akonio lifted his arms high above his head. "Professor al-Qadi!" he shouted. "You were right all along! You always did say I would come to no good!"

"Akonio!"

It was too late. The boy kicked off the minaret and straightened his body into a headlong dive. Like monkey bread from a baobab tree he fell, and like monkey bread he broke open on the ground.

Sheikh Ahmed al-Qadi ibn Abdullah kneeled down next to

the boy. The doctor kneeled on the other side and shook his head. This time there was no need to take a pulse.

Al-Qadi shrugged off his torn outer garment and laid it gently over the body. "Seventeen years old," he murmured. "Am I to blame, doctor?"

"Certainly not. He did this to himself."

"We should bury him straightaway."

"Of course."

"What's a Nommo?"

"I have no idea."

ONE

moktar Hasim smiled to himself. He was on a roll. In the last hour he had scanned three whole manuscripts into the computer, and there was time for yet another before lunch.

He picked up the next manuscript and glanced at the ancient leather cover—another old mathematics treatise from the Abu Bakr collection. Fourteenth century, at a guess. Moktar reached for his keyboard and quickly entered the details: *TMP_172089 / Abu al-Kabari / Introduction to Magic Squares.* He gently undid the leather-lace ties, opened the manuscript to the first page, and lowered the lid of the scanner.

There were two scanners in this department. Moktar's machine stood by the door and his colleague Ahmed's by the window.

"Hey, Mokmok," cried Ahmed. "What are the nine golden rules?"

"Listen up, Dogon," said Moktar. "If you recite the rule book once more, I'll feed it to you."

Ahmed's smile did not fade. He lifted his plump fists in the air and counted on his fingers. "Rule One, keep manuscripts *clean*. Rule Two, do not turn pages *roughly*. Rule Three, do not *slide* manuscripts. Rule Four, do not *lean* on manuscripts. Rule Five, do not *stack* manuscripts. Rule Six—"

"Rule Six, don't call me Mokmok," interrupted Moktar. "Rule Seven, open your scanner. Rule Eight, close your fat Dogon mouth. Rule Nine, do some work for a change. Haven't you noticed that for every manuscript you scan, I scan two?"

"That, my friend, is because you always choose the little ones," said Ahmed, wagging his index finger.

Moktar lifted the heavy lid of his scanner and positioned the next page of his manuscript. The yellowing parchment was as brittle as rice paper, and its edges had been nibbled by termites. *Gently does it,* thought Moktar, lowering the lid. *Don't want to cause any more damage.*

"Stop!" Ahmed's voice in his ear made Moktar jump. "Let me see that."

Moktar whirled round. "Mind your own business! Don't you have any work of your own? Why must you be creeping around and peering over my shoulder like a djinn?"

"Let me look at that page," said Ahmed.

"Look at your own," said Moktar. He turned back to his machine and pressed SCAN.

Ahmed reached over and lifted the lid. "There," he whispered. "In the margin, next to that magic square, someone's done a little drawing."

"Great snakes, you're right!" cried Moktar. "Alert the director! Rouse the mayor! Rally the journalists! I can see the headlines now: SCHOOLBOY DOODLE DISCOVERED IN MATH TEXTBOOK!"

"No need to be sarcastic," said Ahmed. He stepped in front of Moktar and squinted down at the manuscript. "This is incredible," he breathed.

Moktar pushed his colleague aside and took a closer look. The tiny picture wasn't incredible at all. It looked like something a small child would draw—a goggle-eyed fish standing on two little legs.

Ahmed's eyes were shining. "It's the key," he whispered.

"What key? What are you babbling about, man?"

"'It takes a Dogon to know a Nommo,'" quoted Ahmed softly.

It takes a Dogon to know a Nommo. Those weird words stirred a distant memory in Moktar's mind—a legend from the Golden Age of Timbuktu. "What's a Nommo?" he whispered.

Ahmed pointed at the tiny fish-man. "That is," he said. "And I'll bet you a week's wages that this little Nommo was drawn by Akonio Dolo himself."

Akonio Dolo. Moktar remembered the story. Dolo was a Dogon student in Timbuktu who tunneled into a vault beneath the great Sankore mosque and got away with stacks of gold. *Gold that was never found.*

"They found a mathematics manuscript in Dolo's room," said Ahmed, "but they probably didn't give it a second look. And even if they did, who would pay any attention to such a daft doodle? *It takes a Dogon to know a Nommo.*"

Moktar licked his lips. "You think this is the manuscript they found in Dolo's room?" he said.

"Right on, Mokmok." Ahmed hunched low over the manuscript. "Dolo must have drawn the Nommo to highlight this magic square. It's the key, I tell you."

"What key?"

"The key Dolo talked of before he died, the key to the location of the stolen gold. It's what we've all been waiting for, Mokmok. It'll be the find of the century. Two million mithqals! Just think of all the good that could be done with such a—*oof!*"

Moktar brought the heavy lid of the scanner down hard onto his colleague's head, then lifted it again. He yanked the precious manuscript out from under Ahmed's nose and wiped it with his sleeve. The paper was bloody but legible.

"Forgive me, friend," murmured Moktar. "I just broke rules one and three."

Footsteps sounded in the corridor outside. Quick as a flash Moktar dragged the desk in front of the door.

The handle jiggled. "Hello?" It was Austin Wiseman, the American project director. "Ahmed? Moktar? I heard a crash. Are you all right?"

"We're fine," said Moktar. He rolled the parchment tight and put it in his inside jacket pocket.

"Why is this door jammed, Moktar? What's going on?"

Moktar crossed the room quickly, opened the window, and kicked the mosquito netting off the window frame. He began to climb out, then paused. *The computer!* This page of the manuscript had already been scanned. If he wanted sole possession, he had to delete it from the computer.

Wiseman had his shoulder against the door and was shoving hard, prying it open inch by inch. Moktar strode to the computer, seized the mouse, and searched for the newly scanned image.

"Moktar, what are you doing in there?"

Double click. Double click. *TMP_172089/2.*

"Talk to me, Moktar!"

Right click. DELETE.

"Let me in!"

Are you sure you want to delete TMP_172089/2? Yes.

Professor Wiseman was short but strong. He heaved on the door and the barricade gave way. Into the room he rushed, and the first thing he saw was the body of Ahmed Rodin.

Double click. Empty Recycle Bin? Yes.

"Ahmed!" cried the professor, throwing himself down beside the young Dogon and feeling for a pulse. "*Ça va*, Ahmed?"

Moktar strolled to the window and hoisted himself onto the ledge. "So, how is he?"

"Not good," said Wiseman. "What happened here?"

"We found something interesting," said Moktar. "I didn't feel like sharing it."

"What is it?"

"That would be telling."

Wiseman shook his head. "I trusted you, Moktar. I never dreamed you would turn out to be this . . ." He trailed off.

"This what?" said Moktar. "This greedy? This courageous?

This un-Islamic? This imaginative? This what, Professor?"

"This disloyal."

Moktar curled his lip. "My people have a saying, Professor. Loyalty is for contented dogs, discontented wives, and half-contented fools. *Adieu*."

He jumped off the ledge and disappeared from view. An instant later Professor Wiseman reached the window, but his eyes took a moment to adjust to the noonday glare and he did not see which way Moktar had gone. On both sides of the deserted street the glorious mud-brick architecture of Timbuktu shimmered in the sun.

The London HOPE convention was over, and the first surge of youngsters burst out of the Millennium Conference Center and spilled across the forecourt. Most of them wore black T-shirts and carried laptop bags. A group of policemen fidgeted as the black T-shirts passed by; they seemed unsure whether to greet these young people or to arrest them.

Arrest them for what? This crowd was boisterous but not violent, and hacking was not in itself a crime. Besides, the convention was crawling with MI5 agents, scourge of the metropolitan police. Spooks rarely took kindly to being arrested by Police Constable Plod.

In addition to government spooks and corporate spies, the delegates of HOPE included hackers, phone phreaks, cyberpunks, security specialists, journalists, and "simply curious" from all corners of the globe. The hackers themselves comprised white-hat hackers (who used their IT skills only for good), black-hat hackers (virus writers, DOS warriors, and script kiddies), and gray-hat hackers (who hadn't decided which side they were on or didn't recognize any sides at all). This merry band of misfits made up HOPE: Hackers On Planet Earth.

Danny Temple, freelance code monkey, left the building and broke into a jog, tightening the straps on his backpack so that his laptop would not get thrown about. He turned right onto Beaufort Street and made for Battersea Bridge. He was so busy thinking about the events of the day that he did not notice a black Ford Mustang crawling the curb alongside him.

As HOPE conventions went, today's had been a good one. It was kicked off by an American hacker called Isembard Cornell, boasting from the platform about cyberattacks he had launched on various government departments in Whitehall. Some delegates had cheered, others heckled, and the lecture had ended when an egg hit Isembard Cornell on the side of the head. Next up was a closed-circuit TV specialist with a provocative talk entitled "Privacy Is Dead. Deal with It," followed by a Swiss psychiatrist expounding "The Psychology of Hacking." After lunch, delegates had split into groups for the practical workshops. Danny had attended a tutorial on using "rainbow tables" to hack passwords, and he couldn't wait to get back home and try it out.

Arriving at Battersea Bridge, Danny jumped onto the parapet and began to crawl along it on all fours. Below him the River Thames flowed under the bridge toward the sea.

"Are you mad?" shouted a passing cyclist. "One gust of wind and you'll be eating fish."

Worse than that, thought Danny, *my laptop will get ruined.* But he remained calm and balanced; he knew it would take more than a gust of wind to knock him off. He had practiced cat balance on walls and railings all over London before attempting Battersea Bridge. This was parkour, hobby number two, and Danny was no beginner. His friend Omar had taught him well.

At the point where the bridge crossed the South Bank path, Danny stopped, stood up on the rail, swung his arms, and jumped. The time in the air—"hang time," as Omar called it—was as euphoric as ever.

The huge antique lamppost did not even sway when Danny landed on it. He adjusted his grip, slid down, landed lightly on the concrete footpath, and ran. Pedestrians on the bridge gasped in admiration. Adrenaline coursed through Danny's body. Obstacles stretched out in front of him, all of them surmountable.

The South Bank path is parkour paradise—along its length are walls, railings, steps, hedges, bollards, and trees. Open your mind to parkour vision; flow like water over your course. Kong vault, dash vault, tic-tac, kash vault, cat pass, gap jump, dismount, drop. Your will chooses your path, your feeling guides you, your energy propels you.

Parkour is not so very different from hacking. The traceur and the hacker both require special techniques, special vision. Both move freely to surpass the barriers erected by man to enclose and restrict. The electron jungle of cyberspace and the concrete jungle of the city are both there for the exploring—there for the overcoming. Parkour and hacking are about one thing only: freedom.

Danny resisted any big gap jumps on the South Bank path. Big jumps meant hard landings, so he would need to dissipate the shock with a long diagonal roll—left forearm, upper back, lower back, right foot— *"la roulade,"* as Omar called it. An important technique but hardly laptop friendly. Today the smaller, more technical jumps would have to do.

He was approaching Battersea High Street. He ran full speed toward the apartment block on the corner, kicked up off the wall, reached for the railing of an upper-floor balcony, pulled himself up, hopped onto the rail, precision jumped onto a fire escape, and climbed up to the roof.

Danny set his stopwatch to zero, then looked around him and took a deep breath.

Urban monkey. Traceur extraordinaire. *Master of all I survey. I stand on the roofs of Battersea High Street, and before me stretches half a mile of concrete, walls, rails, and chimneys. Chelsea Harbor down to my left, London Eye away to my right. How many days have I run this roof, and in how many different ways? How many nights has my dream self flowed across the city skyline, swan dived over steeples, cat jumped from one skyscraper to the next? How many mornings have I pulled on my running shoes and felt the dizzy thrill of freedom? I'm alive and I'm coming out to play!*

Danny ran across the roofs, vaulting the low walls that separated one flat from the next. If martial arts teach you fight, parkour teaches you flight—an efficient way of evading pursuers and moving smoothly over obstacles in your path. *Kong vault, dash vault, tic-tac, kash vault, cat pass, gap jump, dismount, drop.*

Danny ran quickly and silently, imagining, just for kicks, that he was being pursued.

Danny reached number 185, unlocked a circular skylight, dropped down into the chair below, and pressed his stopwatch—two minutes thirty seconds, not bad. He took the laptop out of his backpack, opened it, and waited for the Wi-Fi to kick in.

Welcome, Danny Temple.
You have **65** new messages.

Danny frowned. He was used to having a full inbox, but sixty-five emails in one morning was a lot even for him. Stranger still, almost fifty of the emails were Facebook friend requests.

He scrolled down through his list of would-be friends. Moira Moran, Ed Potts, Mordecai Kemp. *Ignore, ignore, ignore. I've never even heard of these people. Who are they and why on earth do they suddenly want to be friends with me?*

A sudden sharp knock at the door made Danny look up in surprise. No one ever came to the flat, apart from his friend Omar. And Omar wouldn't knock—he would just walk in. Perhaps it was the landlady.

"Hello. Anybody home?" The visitor's voice was loud and deep. Not the landlady, then.

"Who's there?"

"Opportunity, Danny boy! Opportunity is knocking on your door, so open up."

"Sorry," said Danny. "I don't open up to strangers, even optimistic ones. What do you want?"

"I want to make you rich."

A criminal or a head case, thought Danny. "Go away," he said.

"No. Read this first." A sheet of paper slid underneath the door. It was a printout from a news website.

http://www.afronews.com/stories/200912110039.html

MALI:

Treasure Map Mugger on the Run in Timbuktu

INTER PRESS SERVICE   23 October

Almahady Cissé • Bamako, Mali

Police are searching for twenty-seven-year-old Moktar Hasim, a project worker in the ancient city of Timbuktu. At noon on Thursday Hasim assaulted co-worker Ahmed Rodin and escaped with part of an ancient manuscript, a parchment described by Rodin as a "treasure map."

Professor Austin Wiseman, director of the Timbuktu Manuscripts Project, expressed his surprise and shock at the assault. "Moktar is not a violent man. He behaved out of character and is no doubt regretting his actions. He should give himself up to the police before anyone else gets hurt."

The so-called "manuscript mugger" has now been on the run for two days. Yesterday brought one sighting of him in the Timbuktu animal market, but he escaped before police arrived. Ferrymen on the Niger have been advised to contact the authorities if the fugitive attempts to board a boat going downriver.

Ahmed Rodin, the victim of the assault, was treated for head injuries at the Dispensaire de Timbuktu, where he confided to medical staff the immense value of the stolen document. "It's some sort of map," said the head nurse. "It points the way to a massive stash of lost gold!"

Professor Wiseman was unable to confirm the lost-gold theory. "The fact is we don't know what was taken. The thief not only removed the parchment, he also deleted the digital copy off our hard drive. We look forward very much to the capture of the thief and the opportunity to examine the document for ourselves."

"Well?" said the voice. "Have you finished reading?"

"Yes," said Danny. He put the chain on the front door and opened it a crack. The first thing he saw was an embroidered skull on the lapel of a denim jacket. Then he took in the visitor's unshaven chin, lank curly hair, and pale blue eyes.

"Hello," said the man.

"Who are you?" said Danny.

"Call me Bartholt. I'm a treasure hunter."

"What do you do?"

"Don't act dumb, Danny. A treasure hunter hunts treasure. Detecting, dowsing, digging, diving, whatever it takes."

"You're after that map," said Danny.

"It's the big one, son. Chance of a lifetime. But I need your help to get it."

THREE

Yeah, right." Danny made no attempt to disguise his scorn. "The map is in the hands of a fugitive in Timbuktu. It might as well be buried on the moon."

The treasure hunter shook his head. "Read the article carefully, Danny. There is another copy of the map, isn't there? *There is a copy in the computer.*"

"The digital copy got deleted."

"*Think, you moose!* You know as well as I do that deleting a file is not the same as destroying it. A deleted file hangs around for ages. It stays right where it is and waits to be overwritten. You can retrieve it, can't you?"

"No," said Danny, closing the door. "Not from here."

"I don't believe this!" cried the treasure hunter. "People at HOPE were talking about you like you were some kind of superhero. 'That's Pergamon 256,' they said. 'No system's safe from Pergamon 256.'"

"Sorry to disappoint you," said Danny, double locking the door.

"I get it! You want to hunt that treasure on your own, don't you? You want to cut me out of the loop!"

"Go away!" cried Danny.

"No. We'll do this together or not at all, do you hear me? Hunter and hacker. Knight and nerd. We're the perfect team!"

Danny took a deep breath and bent down to the keyhole. "I'm asking you to leave," he said. "I'm going to count to ten, and if you're still here after that, I'm calling the police. One . . ."

"Leave the police out of this."

"Two . . ."

"Don't play games with me, boy."

"Three . . ."

"Danny!"

"Four . . ."

Silence.

"Five . . ."

Had he gone? Danny bit his lower lip and put his eye to the keyhole.

"Six . . ." Still no sound from the hallway. "Seven . . ."

Danny checked to make sure the chain was still on, then unlocked the door and opened it a chink. The hallway was empty. "Eight . . ." he whispered, his eyes fixed on the top of the stairs, half expecting a horde of loony treasure hunters to appear. But no one came.

"Nine . . ." breathed Danny. He closed the door and double locked it. His knees felt weak, so he let himself slide to the floor, nauseous with relief. Were there really psychotic treasure hunters living in modern-day London? Were there really people called Bartholt? Already the whole encounter seemed to him like something from a dream.

"Ten."

He looked down at the paper in his hand. That was real enough. "Treasure Map Mugger on the Run in Timbuktu"! You couldn't make that up.

"Coming, ready or not!" came a voice from above.

He's on the roof! thought Danny. *I'm dead!*

A shadow fell across the room. As Danny looked up, the glass in the skylight shattered and a chimney pot came crashing through. Instinct made Danny draw his knees up to his chest and cover his face with his hands. Peeking between his fingers, he saw his bed, desk, and floor all covered with shards of glass. Fragments of chimney pot lay around the computer chair, and Bartholt was lowering himself into the room through the smashed skylight. Danny watched him drop to the floor and brush the glass out of his clothes.

The treasure hunter grinned. "Ten," he said. "All these glinting shards are rather pretty, aren't they? Aladdin himself couldn't have wished for a twinklier cave, or Santa for a sparklier grotto. I've made your room a real winter wonderland."

"You're mad," said Danny.

The treasure hunter laughed and rolled his eyes wildly. "Welcome to Narnia!" he cried. "Throw me your phone."

Danny threw it. This was no time for disobedience.

"Thank you." The man pocketed the phone, then went over to the bed and took the pillow out of its case. He placed the pillow on the glass-covered computer chair and motioned Danny to sit down.

"*Voilà,*" said the treasure hunter. He stood behind Danny's chair, still holding the pillowcase. "You have thirty minutes."

"For what?" said Danny.

"For hacking Timbuktu, what else?"

Danny felt sick. He opened a UNIX shell and stared at the command prompt.

"What if I can't do it?" he said.

The treasure hunter shrugged, then brought the pillowcase down over Danny's head. In the darkness, a muffled whisper: "I think you *can* do it, Danny."

The pillowcase came off just as suddenly as it had gone on. Danny sucked in a mouthful of air, blinked rapidly, and put his fingers on the keyboard.

"Just think," whispered Bartholt. "Two million mithqals of gold."

Danny began to feel angry. *Two million mithqals?* he thought. *You're a proper twit, pal. Hack Timbuktu? Sure. The file's been deleted, we don't have a single IP address for Timbuktu, but how hard can it be, right? We'll just nip in behind the firewall, nab the map, hotwire a Land Rover, and mosey on down through the old Sahara to dig up them mithqals, whatever they are. Loot in the boot, we'll be home in time for breakfast. Prat.*

Still fuming inwardly, he began to code.

```c
int main(int argc, char *argv[])
{
    list *l, *new;
    CLIENT *cl;
    int *result;

    if (argc < 2)
        return 1;

    l = new = mk_list("1, timbuktu);
    new = mk_list("2, search);
    new->next = l; l = new;
    new = mk_list("3, available ips);
    new->next = l; l = new;

    cl = clnt_create(argv[1], "tcp");
    }
    result = tunnel_1(l, cl);
    if (result == NULL) {
        printf("error: timbuktu tunnel blocked!\n");
        return 1;
    }
        printf("client: timbuktu tunnel open!\n",
*result);

    return 0;
}
```

"What are you doing?" asked Bartholt.

"I'm implementing an RPC to Timbuktu," said Danny.

"What's an RPC?"

"Remote Procedure Call," said Danny, glancing at Bartholt's reflection in the screen. The treasure hunter's eyes were wide, his cheeks slack with wonder. Danny allowed himself a flicker of hope. *Bartholt knows nothing about UNIX or C+. I'll bamboozle him with a few pages of meaningless code and then use the computer to send an SOS to Omar.*

Five minutes passed. "Any progress?" asked Bartholt.

"Yes," said Danny. "I'm invoking the RPC compiler now."

Five more minutes passed. *Time for that SOS:*

```
int *run RPC_SOS(rpc *lst, struct svc_req *mobile)
{
    list *ptr;

    ptr = lst;
    result = 0;
    mobile (ptr != 0777288628) {
        first=last; last=first
        msg = !ecilop llac !talf ni nam;
    }
    return &result;
}
```

There! Danny ran the code and the SOS was sent. He went on typing, hardly daring to glance at the treasure hunter's reflection in the computer screen. Surely he must have noticed the mobile phone number? Surely the schoolboy cipher could not have fooled him?

Perhaps it had. The incriminating code scrolled out of sight, and still Bartholt said nothing. He stood by Danny's shoulder and gazed at the screen, stupefied by gold lust and technophobia.

He was still standing there eight minutes later when help arrived.

Knock knock. "This is the police. Open the door."

The treasure hunter jumped like a startled gazelle and clapped his hand over his mouth. "No," he whispered through his fingers. "Tell them to go away."

Danny swiveled around to look his adversary in the eye. "Tell them yourself," he said.

Bartholt scowled at the screen, as if still expecting a treasure map to pop up at any moment. Then he gave a deep sigh, deflating visibly as all the air and hope went out of him.

"Stand back!" cried a voice. "We're going to use the battering ram."

"Don't bother," said Bartholt. He stepped quietly to the door and opened it. Two police officers stood on the threshold, and there behind them was Omar "Grimps" Dupont, Danny's best friend in London.

FOUR

One of the policemen led Bartholt out onto the landing for questioning. The other one wandered around
Danny's flat, shaking his head and blowing out his
cheeks.

"Glass everywhere," he said.

Omar rolled his eyes. "No flies on you," he murmured.

The policeman opened a notebook and turned his mournful
gaze on Danny.

"I'll have to file a report," he said. "What is your full name?"

"Daniel Oliver Temple."

"Age?"

"Sixteen," said Danny.

"Do you live here?"

"Yes."

"Which school do you go to?"

"I left school this year."

"You have a job?"

"Yes."

"Good for you. What do you do?"

"Information technology."

"Where do you work?"

"Right here," said Danny. "I freelance."

"Where are your parents?"

"My dad and my stepmum live in Australia."

"Australia?" The policeman frowned. "Why don't you live with them?"

Danny swallowed hard. "I just don't."

"You mean they upped and went?" said the policeman. "Left you here all on your own to fend for yourself?"

"They pay the rent on this place," muttered Danny. *Don't feel sorry for me,* he thought. *You don't know anything about me. I live here and they live there—that's all there is to it. I'm sixteen. I can look after myself.*

The policeman turned a page in his notebook. "Do you know the man outside?"

"No."

"You met for the first time today?"

"Yes."

"Tell me exactly what happened."

Danny told the policeman the whole story and showed him the "Treasure Map Mugger" printout.

"Ah yes," said the policeman, tapping the end of his ballpoint pen on his front teeth. "The famous gold heist of Akonio Dolo."

"You know about it already?" said Danny.

"Yes," said the policeman. "You're not the first HOPE delegate to get attacked today."

Danny jumped at the mention of HOPE. "I'm strictly white-hat," he said.

"Glad to hear it."

"How many hackers have been attacked?"

"Five in the last hour. It seems to be the work of a gang. Or to be more exact, a Facebook group. I'm going to need you to come down to the station tomorrow and give us a statement."

It was over. The police arrested Bartholt the treasure hunter for harassment and criminal damage and took him to the station for further questioning, leaving Danny and Omar to clean up the flat.

"So you got my SOS?" said Danny, kneeling down to brush shards of glass out from under his bed.

"Dan-sel in distress!" Omar chuckled. "I called the police and PK-ed over here straightaway. I took the direct route."

"Not the pygmy goats?" said Danny, laughing. The shortest route between Omar's school and Danny's flat went through the middle of Battersea Park zoo.

"Yes, the pygmy goats. And then the monkeys. I ended up being chased by two attendants and four chimpanzees."

"You got away?"

"I'm here, aren't I?"

"Nice one," said Danny. "Thanks for calling the cops."

"De rien."

Danny was used to his friend slipping into French occasionally, and had picked up from him the French words for many parkour moves. Omar's nickname had come from *grimper,* "to climb" in French, which Danny had heard countless times during practice. Omar's father was French and his mother was English, so he was fluent in both languages. Omar spent term times and half-term breaks at boarding school in London and school holidays with his parents in Paris. This week was half-term, so Omar had plenty of free time.

"Five HOPE-ers attacked in the space of one hour!" said Danny. "What do you make of that?"

"Wild. Who's doing it?"

Danny sat down at the computer. "Plod reckons they're a Facebook group. Let's have a look."

Danny opened his Facebook account, clicked on "Groups," and typed TIMBUKTU in the search box. There were lots of Timbuktu groups, but they all seemed to be about travel or music—nothing about the manuscript mugging. Next he searched for TREASURE HUNTING, and various groups came up.

"It's none of these," said Danny. "These are just kids clowning around with metal detectors."

Omar picked up the news report, which was still lying on the desk. "Try AKONIO DOLO," he said.

Danny ran the search, and there was one result: a group calling itself KNIGHTS OF AKONIO DOLO.

"Woot!" shouted Omar. *Woot* was a hacking expression, a

cry of triumph, which Omar had learned from Danny and now used with annoying regularity.

Danny nodded. "That's got to be them. Bartholt even called himself a knight."

There were forty-eight members of Knights of Akonio Dolo, and the discussion forum was very lively. Topics of conversation all related in some way to Akonio Dolo and the Timbuktu manuscript theft.

"There's your friend," said Omar, pointing to one of the profile pictures. "His name's not Bartholt at all. It's Ronald Smith."

"You're right! And he arranged a Facebook event for today."

"'Bag-a-Hacker,'" read Omar, pronouncing the word in the French way, "ackeur." "'Sunday, October 24. Join our exciting undercover visit to the HOPE (Hackers On Planet Earth) convention. Root out some of the best hackers in London and persuade them to join our treasure hunt. Debrief at 8 p.m. in the Builder's Arms. If you bring the manuscript, drinks are on you!'"

"He made a mistake trying to 'bag' me," said Danny darkly.

"These posts sound innocent enough," said Omar. "I don't think the knights meant to get violent."

"Course they did," said Danny. "Look at their photos, man. Every one of them's an FOC."

"FOC?"

"Face Off Crimewatch."

Omar continued to explore the Facebook group. "Look here," he said, pointing. "It's the story of Akonio Dolo."

Fourteenth-century Timbuktu was a grand old city. It was an important center for the gold trade and also a great place of learning. Scholars came to Timbuktu from all over Africa to study mathematics, religion, astronomy, and law.

The students at Timbuktu University were devout and law-abiding citizens, with the exception of seventeen-year-old mathematics student Akonio Dolo, who was intelligent but dishonest. In 1330, shortly after Mansa Musa's "pilgrimage of gold," Akonio Dolo, a member of the Dogon people of the Macina Region of Mali, planned and carried out the most audacious heist in African history, digging a tunnel under the great Sankore mosque and breaking into a vault that contained over two million mithqals of gold bars—gold donated to the university by Mansa Musa on his return from Mecca.

Working by night for many months, Akonio Dolo visited the vault and stole the gold, working from the back of the vault so that his theft would go unnoticed for as long as possible.

"Cool," said Omar. "He got all that bling completely on his own!"

"Nicking bling isn't cool," said Danny.

"No? What about Robin Hood?"

Danny did not answer. He was already engrossed in the next part of the story.

Akonio Dolo ran out of luck before the vault ran out of gold. Imperial guards found the tunnel and chased the young thief up the wall of the Sankore mosque. Perched on top of the minaret, Dolo confessed to the theft and told his pursuers the location of the stolen gold: a secret chamber in the Dogon cliffs, nineteen ghalva northeast of Tireli. Then he talked of a key that only a Dogon would be able to find. "It takes a Dogon to know a Nommo!" he cried, and with these cryptic last words, he jumped off the minaret to his death.

Immediately Sheikh al-Qadi, high professor of Timbuktu, set off for the Dogon cliffs accompanied by seventy-seven imperial guards. They searched the cliffs all the way from Komokani to Pégué, but returned to Timbuktu without a single mithqal.

The gold of Akonio Dolo has never been found.

Omar punched the air. "Way to go, Dolo my man! You foxed them all good and proper, even that Sheikh Kabaddy fella."

"Al-Qadi."

"Right. Anyway, what's a Nommo when he's at home?"

Danny had asked himself the same question and was already searching the web for the answer. When he found it, he could hardly believe his eyes.

"Nommos are aliens," he said.

"What!"

"They're half man and half fish, and they live on a little planet that orbits the star Sirius B."

"Says who?"

"Say the Dogon people. Looks like the key to Akonio Dolo's secret chamber is a billion light years away in ET's pocket."

Omar frowned, then shook his head. "I don't buy that," he said. "Aliens don't exist. And even if they do, they don't have pockets."

"If you say so," said Danny.

"I do. And anyway, it's far from game over. All you have to do is hack into that Timbuktu computer and find the manuscript, like Bartholt told you to. That's what this is all about, isn't it? The manuscript is the reason why Moktar Hasim went AWOL. The manuscript is the reason forty-eight treasure hunters are wetting themselves with excitement."

"Waste of time," said Danny. "Even the best hacker in the world couldn't recover a deleted file in Timbuktu."

"Really? I thought you used to say that hacking is the same as parkour. Bridging the unbridgeable, cracking the uncrackable, thinking the unthinkable, seeing the invisible. What happened to the parkour vision, bro?"

"I'm just saying it can't be done. I'd explain why, but you wouldn't understand."

"You've lost the magic."

"If you say so," said Danny.

"Pergamon 256, self-styled king of hackers, has given up his throne."

"Whatever." Danny lay down on the bed and closed his eyes. "If I had a few hours to dig around in the Mali network, I could probably root out the Timbuktu Manuscripts Project. But the file we want has been deleted, *comprenez?* It's behind at least two firewalls, and the bits that made it up are probably being over-written already. If we were in Timbuktu, it would be hard enough to recover it, but from here it's impossible. I would need complete remote control of that computer. Nothing less would do."

"Then get it."

"I can't."

"You're chicken."

"Cluck. Shut the door on your way out, will you?"

FIVE

The sun set over Timbuktu harbor, infusing the River Niger with a rich copper glow. A raft was coming downriver, weaving its way among fishermen and their canoes. It jolted suddenly to a stop.

Balanced on the back of the raft, Seydou Zan sighed and plunged his steering pole into the silt below. The raft was the kind of old-fashioned merchant vessel called a pinasse, piled high with merchandise for the people of Timbuktu: canisters of diesel fuel, crates of coal, plastic buckets, bundles of clothes, and sacks of peanuts, sugar, flour, and rice. Zan heaved hard on the end of the pole, but the pinasse did not budge.

"Mud flat!" he cried in a Malian tongue. "Wake up, boys, there's work to do."

Fast asleep on a mound of sugar sacks were two African boys, naked from the waist up. At the sound of the captain's voice, one of the teenagers stirred and grunted in his sleep.

"I said '*Wake . . . up*'!" yelled Zan, emphasizing each word with a vicious blow. As the thwack of steering pole on skin sounded out across the murky river, the boys woke up and leaped off their makeshift beds into the water, one on either side of the pinasse. Half asleep, they fumbled and flailed, calves and triceps straining in the silt.

"Heave!" shouted Zan. "Put your backs into it!"

The river boys dragged the heavy raft off its mud flat. It was common for pinasses to run aground on this river, due to the shallow water and overloaded boats. Mopti to Timbuktu was a three-day journey at best, but extra peanuts and sugar could add a further two days in silt stops. Greedy merchants like Seydou Zan did not mind the delays—why should they? River boys were in plentiful supply and all too willing to do the dirty work in return for a few cigarettes and a fistful of rice.

The pinasse came to rest at the Timbuktu quayside, and Zan stepped off onto solid land. Girls swarmed around him bearing aloft their trays of delicacies: fish, corn, watermelon, chicken legs, and fat-fried dough balls. Zan pushed them aside and strode toward a baobab tree high up on the bank. Behind the tree, the merchant crouched down on his haunches and loosened his string belt.

A twig snapped. Zan turned his head in the direction of the sound and was horrified to see a woman coming up behind him. She wore a burqa, a loose black garment intended to cover a Muslim woman's head and body. The burqa was rare in this part of Africa, but some women used it nevertheless.

"Go away!" croaked the merchant.

The woman did not leave or turn away. She just stood there, looking down at him, head cocked on one side.

"Have you no shame?" cried Zan. "How dare you stand and gawk at me!"

No reply. Maybe the woman did not understand the Bambara tongue.

"Yahu yeeso!" cried Zan in Fulfulde. *"Allez-y!"* he added in French. "Scram!" Perhaps she was a madwoman. Or perhaps— a dreadful thought—she was a *sukunya,* come to eat his soul.

"Salam alaykum, " said the woman, and the gruff voice did not sound like a woman's. Besides, this form of greeting was used only by men. A man in a burqa! Even in these modern times, such a thing was unthinkable.

"Alaykum asalam, " stuttered Zan. "Have you passed the day in peace?"

"Peace only," said the stranger. "Forgive me for creeping up on you whilst your trousers are round your ankles. Shameful of me. Totally un-Islamic."

There was something familiar about the voice. Zan stood up and pulled up his trousers. "I know you," he said slowly. "You once traveled on my pinasse."

The man pulled up the sleeve of the burqa to reveal a shiny silver watch. "And do you know this?" he said.

"My watch!" cried Zan.

"*My* watch," said the man. "I won it off you fair and square, remember?"

Zan did remember. This man had traveled on his pinasse last rainy season. They had come downriver from Mopti to Timbuktu and played cards all the way. The pain of parting with his cherished watch was still raw. What was the man's name again? Mahmud? Malek?

"Thirty-three games of Aztec in four days and four nights." The man chuckled. "You played well, my friend. If you hadn't drunk so much millet beer, you might even have beaten me."

"I remember the game," said the boatman, "but the scoundrel who cheated me out of my watch was a man. He wore a robe and a prayer hat, and when he climbed ashore at Timbuktu, his beard was as long as Abraham's. Definitely a man."

The figure in the burqa took a step closer. "You think me strangely dressed," he whispered. "The truth is, I am in hiding."

"From whom do you hide?"

"From everyone but you."

"Why not from me?"

"Because you own a boat and because you love money. How long before you return to Mopti?"

The boatman shrugged. "However long it takes. I want my raft full to the brim with paying passengers."

"Return tonight," urged the stranger. "Take me with you and I'll pay you well."

Zan wrinkled his nose. "How well?"

"Ten thousand francs."

"Ten thousand francs for taking a fugitive on an empty craft? Only a fool would agree to that. I demand one hundred thousand."

"Forty."

"Eighty."

"Sixty-five."

"Deal," said the boatman. "And one other thing."

"What?"

"I want my watch back."

SIX

The Underground train pulled into Russell Square and Danny got off. The morning rush hour was over, so there was plenty of space on the platform. Space enough to move freely.

"Slow down!" cried an old man as Danny ran past him up the escalator. "You'll do someone a damage."

"*Hey!*" cried a worker as Danny vaulted the ticket barrier. "You can get yourself shot doing that!"

Danny was not in the habit of vaulting ticket barriers, and it was not for lack of a ticket that he did it now, but he was buzzing with energy and excitement. The way he felt, no vault could be too high, no leap too long.

Out into the sunlight he ran, and up the street toward Russell Square Gardens. He remembered these gardens from last summer. He and Omar had passed an idyllic Saturday afternoon here with the Kinetix, the Brixton parkour clan that they sometimes jammed with.

Outside the gardens stood a row of bike stands, ideal for practicing precision jumps. Danny hopped onto the first one and stood motionless with his arms down by his sides. Then he swung his arms, bent his legs, and leaped high into the air. He experienced the familiar adrenaline rush—*The World My Trampoline!*—and then landed feet together on the next bar. His weight was off center and he had to flap his arms to regain balance.

He jumped again, and this time the landing was perfect. Even Baz Dervish, chief of the Kinetix, couldn't have done it better. Danny jumped again and again, making his way all the way to the end of the line and back. *A bad traceur practices a move until he gets it right. A good traceur practices a move until he can't get it wrong.*

Someone hopped up onto the rail next to him. Danny didn't have to look up—he recognized the running shoes.

"Have you tried hacking Timbuktu yet?" said Omar.

"Good morning, Grimps, how are you?"

"Fine, thanks." Omar swung his arms and did a massive precision jump onto the third rail. Typical Omar—always able to go one better, one farther, one higher. He had grown up doing parkour in the Paris suburbs, and he was better than Danny at most of the moves.

"So?" repeated Omar. "Have you tried hacking Timbuktu yet?"

"Yes," said Danny. "I tried last night."

Omar wobbled and fell off his bike stand. "Did you get in?"

"Sort of. I found the computer that hosts the Timbuktu Manuscripts Project, and I tried to access the departmental file server."

"And?"

"I ran smack into Smoothwall."

"What's that?"

"A network firewall."

"So what did you do?"

"I boarded up the skylight instead."

"Oh." Omar's face fell. "Gutted."

"Come on," said Danny. "Let's run."

Danny jumped off his rail and sprinted away up the street, but Omar was a faster runner and soon caught up. They ran through Russell Square Gardens, practicing kong vaults over the park benches.

"Look," said Omar. "There's our friend the duke!"

The illustrious Fifth Duke of Bedford was commemorated by a statue on the south side of the gardens close to a row of chestnut trees. When the Kinetix had come here last summer, the old duke's statue had captured their imagination. They had spent a good half hour swinging from tree to tree, precision jumping onto the duke's statue, and dismounting with a roll. It had been the highlight of the Russell Square jam.

"Anyway," said Danny, "when I went to bed last night, I couldn't sleep. I was totally wired, what with HOPE and the break-in and Timbuktu and all. So I was just lying there racking my brains, and suddenly I had an idea. What's the worst thing about living in Timbuktu?"

"Heat stroke."

"No."

"Sand in your sandwiches."

"No."

"What then?"

"The phone bills! Poor old Professor Wiseman must pay a fortune every time he calls America. Unless . . ."

"Unless he's running Skype," said Omar.

"Exactly," said Danny. "And since Austin Wiseman isn't the most common name in the world, it took me about two seconds to find his Skype account."

"So what?"

"So that was my way in. For most people, the good thing about Skype is that it enables you to make incredibly cheap long-distance calls. But for hackers, the good thing about Skype is that it can walk through firewalls. If you can trick your target into installing a specially written plug-in on their computer, you can use Skype as a back door to gain complete control. So I hid the plug-in on a spoof web page and emailed the link to all the workers in the Timbuktu Manuscripts Project."

"And?"

"And then I went to sleep."

They ran out of the park and up Thornhaugh Street, dodging pedestrians and tic-tac-ing off the wall—using the side of the wall as a springboard to gain height or change direction. It was one of Danny's favorite moves.

"Well?" said Omar. "Did anyone click on the link?"

"One person must have," said Danny. "Because at exactly six forty-five this morning I was woken up by a Skype call all the way from Timbuktu! It was the central computer at the Manuscripts Project, and it was basically calling to say 'Hello, make me a zombie!' From then on it was easy. I accessed the departmental file server, mapped the network drive through the Skype tunnel to my computer, and ran an undeletion tool."

"And?" Omar was agog. "Was the treasure map there or not?"

"Yes, it was."

"Woot!" Omar rugby tackled Danny and pinned him to the pavement. "Why didn't you say so ten minutes ago, dingbat! Let me look at it!"

Danny laughed and took from his back pocket a piece of paper. "Here you go," he said. "One Timbuktu treasure map."

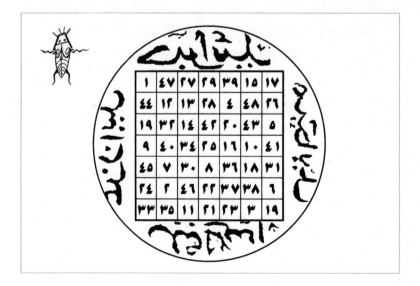

Omar was quiet for a few seconds and then said, "That's the rubbishest treasure map I've ever seen."

"Oh yeah?" said Danny. "How many treasure maps have you seen?"

"You know what I mean. I thought it was going to be a street plan of Timbuktu."

"'X marks the spot?'"

"At least I could understand that."

"Sorry, Grimps. Very inconsiderate of them to leave off the X."

"It's not just the X, man! They've left off the whole map! And then a schizoid spider has come along and done a sudoku on it."

"It's Arabic."

"It's 'ad a bit, if you ask me. How do you even know it's the right manuscript?"

"Look again at the margin," said Danny.

Omar looked. "So what?" he said. "Some douchebag's drawn a two-legged fish."

"Otherwise known as a Nommo," said Danny.

"Oh, yes!" Omar brightened up suddenly.

"That Nommo is the reason Moktar Hasim stole the manuscript," said Danny. "He must have realized that it was Akonio Dolo's way of drawing attention to this square."

"In that case," said Omar, "all we need now is someone who knows a bit of Arabic and can interpret the square for us."

"I've found someone already," said Danny. "His name's Robin Redvald, and he's a history student at SOAS, the London School of Oriental and African Studies. I emailed him to ask his help."

"You didn't tell him it's a treasure map, did you?"

"Of course not."

"And where is this School of Oriental What-you-said?"

"Over there." Danny pointed to a large redbrick building across the street. "There's a Japanese garden on the roof. We're meeting Redvald there in ten minutes."

SEVEN

The boys entered the School of Oriental and African Studies and climbed the steps to the roof garden. No one else was there.

The Japanese-style garden was elegance itself. A swath of light gray granite chippings ran like a river through the center of the garden, with darker gray stones placed here and there to form bridges and islands. At the source of the granite river a checkerboard of slate and earth had been planted with herbs and tiny colored windmills, and at the other end was a low wooden stage covered by a pergola. The whole garden was enclosed by a high wall.

Omar sat down on the edge of the stage and gazed up at the lattice of vines and purple flowers above his head. *"Magnifique,"* he said. "I feel calmer already."

Danny looked at his watch. "It's ten o'clock. Where's Red-vald?"

"Relax, *mon ami.*"

"That's easy for you to say. You're not the one with a price-less manuscript in your pocket."

Omar did a handstand in the center of the stage and grinned at Danny upside down. "Chill out, bro. The world is very big and your problems are very small."

The door to the roof garden opened and a young man stepped blinking into the sunlight. He wore brown corduroy trousers and a blue jacket.

"Hello," said Danny. "Are you Robin Redvald?"

"Yes."

They shook hands.

Omar did a handspring and landed on his feet. "Nice place you've got here, Robin, my man. Making me feel dead calm."

"It's the stones," said Redvald. "See those big gray ones in the middle there? They're larvikite. When you go near them, your blood pressure drops."

"Cool," said Omar.

"Larvikite opens up your mind, too," said the student. "Helps you understand complicated facts and make good decisions."

"Do you really believe that?" said Danny.

"Me and one hundred million Japanese people."

"Fair enough." Danny sat down on one of the stones, and Robin Redvald sat next to him.

"You said in your email that you have some Arabic you want me to translate for you?" he said.

"Here." Danny handed him the page.

"Where did you get it?"

"Found it on the net," said Danny. "It's a scanned copy of some old manuscript or other."

"Nice," said the student. "Looks like it's from Timbuktu."

"How do you know?"

"The Timbuktu libraries are home to thousands of Africa's ancient manuscripts. Judging by the style of the lettering, this is one of them."

Danny glanced at Omar, who was crouching next to the historian, listening intently.

"The Timbuktu manuscripts are essentially toast," continued Redvald. "They are being slowly baked by the Sahara, and they provide breakfast, lunch, and tea for trillions of termites. Professor Wiseman in Timbuktu wants to preserve the contents of the manuscripts, and he has persuaded various library owners to let his team scan them. It's all rather exciting—a race against time, you might say. The team has to save all the manuscripts to disk before the parchments turn to dust."

"Good for them," said Danny. "What does this one say?"

Redvald put on a pair of glasses and studied the manuscript. "Each box in the grid contains an Arabic number."

"Told you it was a sudoku," hissed Omar.

"Not quite," said Redvald. "It looks to me more like a magic square. Every row, column, and diagonal adds up to the same total, and no number is used twice. Magic squares are used a lot in West Africa for making amulets and codes."

"Good thing I'm sitting on larvikite," said Omar. "I'd be lost otherwise."

Redvald ignored the sarcasm. "This one's a beauty," he murmured. "Seven columns, seven rows, and the names of the four archangels written along the sides: Gabriel, Michael, Israfil, and Azrail. All in all, it's a classic example o——"

The history student broke off in midsentence and peered at the paper more closely. When he looked up, there was suspicion in his eyes.

"Where did you get this?" he said.

EIGHT

Danny groaned inwardly. He'd known Redvald would be able to translate the Arabic, but hadn't expected him to recognize the Nommo for what it was.

"I told you," he said evenly. "We found it on the net."

"Where on the net?" Redvald's gaze was cold and unblinking.

"I don't remember."

"Rubbish!"

Danny tried to take back the paper, but Redvald whisked it up out of reach.

"Cool it, guys," said Omar. "Let's just sit down on our larvikite, shall we, and wait for the old blood pressure to drop."

"Give that back!" yelled Danny.

"No!" said Redvald. "You've got a nerve, bringing this here."

"Islands of serenity," intoned Omar. "Seas of tranquility. Windmills, lemon thyme, calm, calm, calm."

"Just this morning our history professor told us about a crime that took place in Timbuktu a few days ago," said Redvald. "A Dogon scholar was working in the scanning department of the Timbuktu Manuscripts Project when he noticed a little doodle in the margin of a mathematics textbook. It takes a Dogon to know a Nommo, isn't that right, Danny?"

"Give me back my manuscript!"

"His colleague coshed him and stole the document. Not a very nice man, eh, Danny?"

"Give it back!"

"Is Danny your real name, Danny? Have you been in contact with a man called Moktar Hasim, Danny? Did he send you here?"

"I don't know what you're talking about."

"Liar!" Redvald stood up as if to leave.

Danny panicked. Before he knew what he was doing, he had elbowed the student in the mouth and snatched the treasure map out of his hand.

"Oh no," sighed Omar. "Now you've done it."

Robin Redvald stared in shock and a tiny trickle of blood dribbled down his chin. *"Help!"* he yelled. *"Security! Come quick!"*

Danny dived through the door and made for the stairs, quickly followed by Omar, but it was already too late. A burly security guard was coming up from below, taking the steps three at a time.

The boys dashed back out onto the roof, but Redvald was waiting for them, brandishing a long piece of larvikite.

"Peace!" cried Omar, backing away with his hands up. "Tranquility! Harmony!"

The security guard arrived, breathing heavily after his swift ascent. "What's going on here?" he said.

Redvald stepped forward and showed his student ID card. "These thugs just assaulted me," he said, "and they are in possession of a valuable stolen manuscript."

The guard licked his lips and moved toward the boys. "All right, lads," he said. "Come with me."

Danny caught his friend's eye and raised an eyebrow. Omar nodded. It was not worth trying to explain. Escape was clearly the best policy.

Omar was first to move. He hopped up onto one of the stone islands and then jumped from rock to rock, gathering speed as he went. The guard tried to intercept him, but Omar was too quick. He crane jumped onto a tall water basin and leaped for the wall.

"Go, Grimps!" shouted Danny.

Omar grabbed the parapet and hung there a moment, gathering his strength. Then, in one explosive move, he pulled himself all the way up onto the top of the wall.

The guard kicked over the water basin and turned to face Danny. "What about you?" he said. "Got any tricks up your sleeve?"

Danny looked at the wall and compared it in his mind's eye to jumps he had done before. *A traceur knows intuitively if he is able* to execute a move. *Doubt is his friend, not his enemy.* Without the water basin as a kickoff, the wall was simply too high.

Redvald sneered. "What's wrong, Danny? Has monkey boy escaped and left you in your cage?"

The two men opened their arms wide and began to advance. Danny stepped onto a slab of larvikite in the middle of the garden and looked left and right. *Parkour vision is an illness*—la maladie du traceur. *When you start to parkour, you begin to see things differently. You see alternative paths to your objective. The longer you practice, the more paths you see.*

Robin Redvald was approaching on Danny's left. The guard was on the right, fingers reaching out to grab his collar.

The pergola.

Danny ducked and bolted through the small gap between the two men. He ran the length of the garden, kicked up off the low stage, and grabbed hold of the trellis overhead. It groaned under his weight and released a shower of purple flowers over the stage. Danny changed his grip and began to wriggle up through the trellis.

"No, you don't!" snarled the guard, but it was too late. By the time the pursuers reached the pergola, Danny's feet were disappearing between the slats.

"Help!" yelled Redvald. *"They're getting away! Stop them!"*

Danny precision jumped onto the wall and cat balanced along the top of the parapet toward Omar. His friend was leaning over the side of the building, looking for a way down.

"Hey, Danny," said Omar. "You remember the multistory car park on Queen's Road?"

"Yes."

"And the south chimney at Battersea Power Station?"

"Yes."

"Tricky descents, weren't they?"

"Yes."

"Well, so is this. But don't worry, you'll be fine."

Omar turned around and bent down as if to touch his toes. He gripped the parapet and shuffled his feet a little way down the face of the wall. Danny realized what his friend was about to do—he was going to drop down onto a fourth-floor window ledge, a strip of wood no more than six inches wide.

"Don't do it, Grimps."

Omar dropped. The balls of his feet landed on the narrow ledge and he grabbed the window frame to catch himself. Then he bent down and prepared for the next drop. Typical Omar—never gave himself time enough to panic.

Danny crouched, held on to the wall, and moved his feet into position. He watched his knuckles whiten on the parapet, and again his mind flashed back to Battersea Power Station. A couple of months before, Baz, the leader of the Kinetix, had climbed the south chimney of the power station, and Danny had gone up after him because he wanted to impress the girls. But when Danny had reached the top of the chimney and looked down, his initial euphoria had turned to dread. Climbing a tall building took strength; going down took guts.

Omar was now at the third-floor window, leaving Danny clear to jump. "Here goes," breathed Danny. *Fall like a cat.* He let go of the wall and landed on the fourth-floor window ledge. It was all wrong—he was totally off balance. Frantic fingernails scrabbled on the windowpane. He fell off.

What had Omar said to him that day in the car park? *Keep your hands on the wall, even in free fall. The friction will slow you down.* As Danny fell, he reached out to brush the rough bricks in front of him. He landed hard on the next ledge and grabbed the frame to catch himself. His knees smacked the windowpane, and it cracked from corner to corner.

"You okay, Danny?" shouted Omar.

"No!" shouted Danny.

"There's a grip down there on your right."

Sure enough, there was a college crest bolted to the wall high above the entrance to the building. It looked sturdy enough. Danny jumped toward it and winced as his sore palms made contact with the rough cast iron.

"Too tense!" shouted Omar, who was already on the ground. "Loosen up. Flow along your course."

Danny hung from the SOAS crest and took deep breaths to calm himself. He was staring straight ahead at an engraving of a camel and an elephant, both standing on their hind legs. They held a coat of arms between them, and around their legs there curled a scroll that bore three words: KNOWLEDGE IS POWER.

Danny clambered across the crest and jumped toward the next window ledge. He landed with one foot on the ledge, dropped down to swing on it, chose his spot on the lawn below, and let go. This was a big jump, and he was shocked at how quickly the grass rushed up to meet him.

"*Roulade!*" cried Omar.

Danny landed on the lawn, bent his knees, and rolled forward—hands, shoulders, back, backside, foot. It was a good roll and hardly hurt at all.

Someone was shouting. It was the security guard, leaning out of a fourth-floor window and pointing at Danny and Omar. "Stop them!" he cried. "Stop, thieves!"

Several passersby had stopped to watch the boys' daring antics on the face of the SOAS building. One or two had even applauded Danny's successful dismount. But when the crowd heard the guard's shouts, admiration turned quickly to alarm. One or two started forward toward the boys and then stopped. Did they really want to get mixed up in this? After all, maybe these crazy acrobats were carrying.

Four Chinese students were exercising on the lawn not far from where Danny had landed. As soon as they realized what was happening, they raised their fists and rushed toward Danny and Omar. One of them let out a ferocious cry that sounded like "*Zougou!*"

"Come on, Danny!" Omar was tugging at his sleeve. "Time for a run!"

NINE

ACROSS the SOAS forecourt they ran, past the elm trees, the bicycle racks, and the student union, hotly pursued by the four Chinese boys.

Omar was grinning wildly. "This is what it's about, Danny," he said. "This is what we train for."

"Glad you're enjoying yourself," said Danny, but in truth he was getting exactly the same rush. Now that they were down on solid ground, they were back in control, and all those hours of running and vaulting practice were about to pay off.

They ran past Senate House and sprinted straight across the street without looking. Danny was only halfway across when he saw the vast red frontage of a Number 16 bus bearing down on him. *Trust a hacker to get himself killed by a hexadecimal bus.*

The driver braked sharply and sounded his horn, and Danny made it to the sidewalk by a whisker. The Chinese boys stopped to let the bus go past and then took up the chase again.

On into Russell Square they ran. It was lunchtime, and the

park was busier than it had been earlier. Students, lovers, dog walkers, crossword solvers, everyone was out enjoying the greenery, the exotic flower beds, and the peaceful shade of the chestnut trees.

"*Zougou*—running dog! Stop, thief!"

Danny turned to see one of the Chinese students tearing up the path behind them.

Where are the other three?

The park was crisscrossed by two long diagonal paths, meeting in the center at a playful fountain. The boys headed straight for it.

"Our Chinese friends have split up," panted Omar. "They must have gone on along the outside of the railings. They're going to surround us."

Danny turned and sized up his pursuer. "Enough running," he muttered to Omar. "Let's double back and give *Zougou* here a kung fu lesson."

Omar slowed to a jog and stopped on the far side of the fountain, scowling. "You're a traceur, Danny, so stop talking like a happy-slapper. Don't make the same mistake twice."

"What are you carrying on about?"

"Robin Redvald. You asked his advice and then thumped him in the gob!"

"He had our map!" said Danny.

"That map has turned you into a real prat."

"Is that your expert diagnosis?"

"Yes."

"Well, here's mine," said Danny. "I've got a copy of the most talked-about document in the world right here in my pocket. A magic square encrypting the location of two million mithqals of gold. So excuse me if I think that's something worth protecting."

The Chinese student had caught up with them and taken up a position just the other side of the fountain. Straight black hair poked out from under a Chicago Bears baseball cap. "Citizen's arrest!" he shouted.

A young couple on a nearby bench broke off in midkiss and turned their heads in alarm.

"Keep the fountain between him and us," said Omar. "And whatever you do, don't let him touch you."

"Why not?"

"Those movements they were doing on the lawn back at SOAS. Looked to me like dim mak. The touch of death."

"That was tai chi," said Danny. "You're the only dim mak around here, Grimps."

The other three Chinese lads came into view, taking up their positions at the exits. High iron railings ran all around the park, topped with cruel spikes.

"I hate to say this," whispered Danny, "but we're trapped."

Omar pulled a face. "What happened to your vision, bro? A traceur is never trapped. Look how close to the railings the Duke of Bedford is."

Danny looked, and a grin spread slowly across his face. "It'll be just like old times," he said.

That grin provoked their pursuer into attacking. Danny had

expected him to try to come at them round the fountain, but instead he bounded straight through it. Wet through and livid, he jumped out of the pool and flung himself at Danny and Omar.

"*Zougou!*"

Danny reached the first chestnut tree just ahead of his friend, kicked off the trunk, and pulled himself up into the branches. It was just like last summer, jamming with the Kinetix. The chestnut trees felt like old friends.

What followed was a classic underbar sequence, the kind Omar called *lache*. Danny built his speed from branch to branch, and his momentum off the last tree took him all the way onto the duke's statue. A soft rain of chestnuts pattered onto the grass below as the branch sprang back into place.

The Fifth Duke of Bedford was a keen farmer, and his statue depicted him with a sheep and a plow at his feet. Danny precisioned onto the duke's pedestal, tic-tac-ed up the sheep and plow, and then launched himself high into the air.

Hang time was delicious. Danny brought his knees up under his chin, sailed over the iron railings, and came down on top of a Volvo that was parked in the street outside the gardens. He rolled down the hood and landed softly on the asphalt. An imaginary crowd applauded wildly.

Omar's dismount was even more spectacular. He cleared the railings in a perfect swan dive, smacked his knee on a parking meter, and crumpled onto the sidewalk.

"Grimps!" Danny kneeled by his friend. "Are you all right?"

Omar sat up and blinked hard. "How was that for a bail?"

"Awesome," said Danny. "How do you feel?"

"My knee's killing me."

"Can you walk?"

"I don't know."

"The Triads will be coming after us any minute, so try!"

Omar got up, hobbled a few paces, and stopped. "Ouch," he said.

Danny put an arm round Omar's shoulder, and together they hurried across the street like contestants in a three-legged race. Large terraced houses towered over the sidewalk.

"We need to get off the street," said Danny. "Watch out for anyone opening a door."

"There! What about him?"

An old man had turned off the sidewalk just ahead of them and was climbing the steps toward the door of an ornate town house. He began to tap a security code into the keypad by the door.

Danny arrived at the bottom of the steps just as the old man disappeared into the shadowy interior. He bounded up the steps and put his toe in the gap to stop it from closing.

"Get a move on, Grimps," urged Danny, looking up and down the street.

Omar hobbled up the steps and through the door. Danny slipped in too and closed it gently behind them.

TEN

Danny and Omar found themselves in a high-ceilinged hallway. There were two doors leading off it and a staircase going up. No family photos, no coat rack, no children's toys, nothing to indicate that people actually lived here. Danny peeked through a keyhole and saw the old man they had followed in; he was shuffling along a bare corridor lined with doors. This was no family home.

"Do you think the Dim Mak Pack saw us?" asked Omar, peeking out through the letter slot.

"I don't know. I think we should try to roof it from here, though, just in case. How's your knee?"

"Sore," said Omar. "Don't expect me to do any more swan dives in the next five minutes."

They climbed one flight of stairs and came to a large bank of pigeonholes on the landing. Danny picked an envelope at random. "Jacques Khalil," he read. "Keeper of Antiquities."

"Oh goody," said Omar. "We've stumbled into the headquarters of a secret society. Let me guess: Opus Dei? Priory of Sion?"

Danny looked at another envelope. This one was addressed to the Egyptology Department.

Egyptology. Antiquities. Montague Place. Danny suddenly realized where they were. "This isn't a secret society," he said. "It's part of the British Museum. These must be staff offices!"

Omar groaned. "We are *so* trespassing."

"Don't worry, Grimps. We'll be up on the roof in no time."

They went up two more flights of steps and came to a door marked AUTHORIZED PERSONNEL ONLY. Danny grinned and reached for the handle. *"Mesdames et Messieurs,"* he said. *"Voilà* Escape Route A."

The handle did not budge. The door was double locked.

"Nice try," said Omar. "What's Escape Route B?"

"The corridors," said Danny, making it up as he went along. "I'm guessing that they all lead into the public galleries of the museum. Once we're through, we can mingle with the crowds and leave through the main doors."

"You're joking," said Omar. "We're going to just stroll down the corridor like we own the place?"

"It's called physical hacking," said Danny. "Moving about in places you're not supposed to be in. Cracking security doors, getting past receptionists, picking locks, chatting up cleaners, strolling down corridors like you own the place. It's all about confidence, mate. Just follow me and do what I do."

They went downstairs and started along a brightly lit corridor.

Omar hobbled as fast as he could, and Danny walked behind him, reading the names on the various offices they passed. PREHISTORY, MIDDLE EAST, COINS AND MEDALS, AFRICA, MAPS AND DRAWINGS. There was a small glass panel in each door, and Danny could not resist the occasional peek. Some of the offices were in use, others seemed to be empty.

"That was some good *lache* back there," whispered Danny. "We flowed like water."

"I flowed like a brick into that parking meter," whispered Omar. "I'm lucky I didn't break my kneecap or someth—"

He stopped dead. *What was that?* A sound had come from the door at the far end of the corridor. *The sound of a key in a lock.*

"In here, Grimps!" Danny dived into an empty office on his left, and Omar hobbled in after him. The office smelled of sweat and furniture polish.

"What happened to Mr. Confident?" said Omar. "What happened to Mr. Physical Hacking? Mr. Just Stroll down the Corridor?"

"He's taking a break," said Danny.

The bookshelves lining the office were crammed with books, and a solid wooden computer desk stood by the window.

"I can hear footsteps," hissed Omar. "And voices. They're heading right for this office."

"Quick! Round the back of the desk!"

They squeezed between the desk and the window and crouched down.

"You're too high, Grimps. Lie lower."

"I can't."

"You have to. Your bum is waving in the air."

"If I get any lower, your foot will be in my face."

"Think of it as fine Camembert."

"You're cruising for a dim mak-ing."

"*Shhh.*"

The door opened and two people came into the office.

"Prince Mukenze," said a reedy voice, "you have my fullest sympathy. But please understand the delicacy of our situation."

The second voice sounded African. "I do not want your sympathy, Mr. Curator. I want the bronze statuettes. They are vital to the religious life of my nation."

"But they have been in the possession of the British Museum for over a hundred years."

"You stole them! You torched our royal palace, exiled our king, and stole our bronzes."

"I did nothing of the sort!"

"The guilt of your great-grandfathers is on your head, Mr. Curator, and the rage of King Ovonramwen is in my heart."

"In that case, I would advise you to address your concerns in writing to the secretary of the museum. He will send you an RRR as soon as possible."

"What is an RRR?"

"Request for Repatriation of Relics."

"There is a form for that?"

"Indeed there is." The curator gave a nervous laugh. "We can't print enough of them these days."

"*Mister* Curator." The prince's voice shook with anger. "Do you know how many miles it is from Lagos to London?"

"Three thousand?"

"Three thousand *and ninety-eight*. I did not fly all this way to be fobbed off with empty words."

"Oh dear. Then how about I print you out a form and you can fill it in here and now?"

Danny heard the whir and chunter of a hard drive as the computer on the desk booted up. His toes were cramping. He longed to stand up and jump around.

There was a strained silence while the curator tapped in his password and printed out the form. Danny held his breath. Then at last the prince spoke again.

"You did not tell me the RRR was so long."

"It is good and thorough," said the curator. "The museum's repatriation board needs as much detail as possible in order to judge your claim."

"Judge my claim?" cried the African prince. "You expect Oba Mukenze to bow before a bunch of bleating British bureaucrats? You can roll up your RRR and swivel on it."

"Prince Mukenze, please!"

"You will be hearing from our lawyers. Goodbye."

Danny heard the slam of a door, then indistinct curses and hurrying footsteps in the corridor outside. The prince had clearly taken his leave with great panache. *Exit, pursued by a curator.*

The boys raised their heads cautiously, then jumped up and stretched their aching limbs.

"'Bow before a bunch of bleating British bureaucrats!'" sang Omar. "Try saying that with a marshmallow in your mouth!"

Danny went to the door and turned the handle. "Oh no," he said.

"What?"

"We're locked in."

ELEVEN

Moktar Hasim was tired but dared not sleep. He sat hunched at the back of the pinasse, knees drawn up under his chin, gazing out across the water. For the first time in his life, he was a fugitive from the law, and anxiety was driving him out of his mind. Under his burqa he carried the most valuable document in Africa, a manuscript that many men would kill for.

Emptied of almost all its cargo, the merchant vessel sat high in the water and moved upriver at a good pace. In the fourteen hours since leaving Timbuktu they had hardly got stuck at all; at this rate they would reach Mopti in three days.

Seydou Zan, the boatman, slumped at the opposite end of the pinasse, fast asleep against a large sack of dates. His left arm hung over the side of the boat and his fingertips trailed in the water. There was the slightest hint of a smile at the corner of his mouth.

Moktar glanced upriver and down. There were no other

boats in sight, and the banks of the river were silent, save for the occasional sharp cry of a water bird. There was only one river boy in the boat for this journey. He was steering the craft well enough, but like the boatman, he had hardly said a word since leaving Timbuktu. It was the silence that made Moktar uncomfortable—so different from last year's journey, when they had argued and played cards and drunk millet beer all the way to Timbuktu. Why this terrible silence now?

He felt underneath his burqa for the scroll. Yes, there it was, safely tucked into his belt. Possession of that scroll was what made everything worthwhile. The silence, the loneliness, the nagging guilt, the discomfort of this long journey to Mopti, even the indignity of his disguise. When the treasure of Akonio Dolo was finally in his grasp, all this would be nothing but a bad dream.

What was that? He could have sworn that Zan's right eyelid had just flickered. Was Zan really asleep or just pretending? Moktar withdrew his hand slowly from his burqa and scanned the boatman's face. The strange smile was still there—and yes, look at that!—the eyelids were not entirely closed. Or were they? It was impossible to tell at this distance. Moktar looked away and back again. He was sure of it now—under half-closed lids, the boatman was watching him. Moktar's skin began to crawl.

Why was the boatman watching him so intently? Maybe he was still sulking about last year's card game. Or wondering what kind of man pays sixty-five thousand francs for a single boat ride. *Or perhaps*—horrible thought!—*perhaps he knows!*

Perhaps he's already heard about the manuscript mugging and has realized who I am. In which case, he knows what I'm hiding under my burqa!

Moktar hugged his knees closer to his body and pulled his veil down over his face. Two and a half days to go until Mopti. He could not possibly last two more nights without sleep. But if he fell asleep, what then? Surely that was exactly what the boatman was waiting for. *A sleeping man is child's play to rob.*

Beads of sweat formed on Moktar's forehead. *He's as sly as a snake, that Seydou Zan—I should never have come on this accursed boat. I should have tried to get to Mopti overland. I should have hijacked a truck. I should have waylaid some goggle-eyed tourist and forced him to drive for me. I should have crossed the border into Burkina Faso and lain low for a few months. I've played my hand all wrong, and now I'm paying the price. I'm stuck in a boat with a poisonous snake who's pretending to sleep but is really awake, who's biding his time, preparing to strike, preparing to bite me and swipe my golden egg. Hear my prayer, O Merciful and Compassionate One, and get me off this boat. Get me away from this vicious, treacherous, venomous man, and let me get that gold!*

TWELVE

The boys crouched behind the desk and waited for the curator to come back. Where on earth had he gone? Lunch? A meeting across town?

Danny counted the minutes. Five. Ten. Twenty.

"I just want to be FREE!" sang Omar suddenly, jumping up to stretch his arms and legs.

"Get *down*," hissed Danny. "Someone will see you."

But Omar did not listen. He strolled to the window and examined the fastenings.

"Grimps," ordered Danny, "come back here. The curator could come back any minute."

"Double locked," muttered Omar, but then he noticed something else. He grinned and pointed up at the ceiling. "Looky here, Danny boy! It's Mr. Smoke Detector."

"So what?" said Danny.

"Here's the plan," said Omar, fishing in his pocket. "We light a match right under the detector here, the alarm goes crazy, twenty firefighters rush in shouting 'Where's the fire?,' and in the confusion we slip quietly out the door."

Omar was not a smoker, but he always carried matches with him. His parents stayed at the Paris Ritz and gave him the matchbooks as souvenirs. He opened one now and broke off a match.

"If you light that," said Danny, "we'll both be arrested for trespassing."

"We'll be fine, mate."

"Maybe, maybe not," said Danny. "Just don't come moaning to me when our heads are on spikes on Tower Bridge."

Omar seemed to waver but then put the matches back in his pocket. "Have you got a better idea, O Wise One?"

"Yes," said Danny. "We find out how long we're stuck here for."

"And how do you propose we do that?"

"We read Mr. Curator's diary, which I'm guessing is in his computer here."

Danny got stiffly to his feet and opened up Diary Manager on the curator's desktop PC. Sure enough, the diary showed various engagements, including the meeting with Prince Mukenze of Nigeria. The last entry for the day said simply "12:30 p.m.— the Valley."

"Grimps, what's the Valley?"

"Charlton Athletic football ground. Please don't tell me he's gone to the Valley."

"He's gone to the Valley."

"Is he coming back here afterward?"

"I shouldn't think so."

"Well," said Omar. "I hope his team loses, that's all I can say."

Danny did not reply. He went over to the bookshelves and ran a finger along the spines of the curator's books, stopping at a thick black one with gold lettering: *Classical Arabic: A Reference Grammar*. He slid the book toward him and blew a fine layer of dust off the top.

"Let me guess," said Omar. "You're thinking about your square."

"Yup," said Danny. "Seeing as we're stuck here all afternoon, we may as well do something useful. Knowledge is power, remember?"

He rummaged on the curator's desk for a piece of scrap paper and drew a seven-by-seven grid. Then he flicked through the grammar book until he came to the section on Arabic numerals.

"Nice," muttered Omar. "One square working on another."

Like most hackers, Danny was obsessed with codes and code breaking. Right now he felt as if this puzzle was a personal challenge set for him by Akonio Dolo. Working quickly but carefully, he translated the Arabic numbers into English and wrote them into his empty grid.

1	47	27	29	39	15	17
44	12	13	28	4	48	26
19	32	14	42	20	43	5
9	40	34	25	16	10	41
45	7	30	8	36	18	31
24	2	46	22	37	38	6
33	35	11	21	23	3	19

"Give us a look," said Omar. "I'll finish your sudoku before you can say bleating bureaucrats."

Danny totted up the numbers in the first few rows and columns. "Sweet," he said. "The numbers in each line total 175!" He began to surf the net on the curator's computer, reading everything he could find about magic squares and African cryptography. "'The square of order seven is associated with the planet Venus,'" he read aloud. "'Engraved on a silver plate and placed in a hen coop, the square increases egg production. Carried by a traveler, it produces good fortune.'"

"One hundred seventy-five grams!" said Omar suddenly. "That's the regulation weight for an Ultimate Frisbee!"

"You think Akonio Dolo was thinking about Ultimate Frisbee when he coded this square in Timbuktu seven hundred years ago?"

"Maybe not." Omar closed his eyes and furrowed his brow. "Wait—wasn't Flight 175 one of those hijacked planes on 9/11?"

"Good point. I guess the gold must be in New York. Go and have a look for it, there's a good Grimps. And while you're at it, pick me up a hot dog."

"Funny man," muttered Omar. "What do you think it means, then?"

"I think it's gematria," said Danny, still clicking from page to page. "Each number in the grid represents a letter. Read the grid in the right direction and it will spell out the name of a village or settlement or something."

"How do you know which number stands for which letter?"

"I don't," said Danny. "But give me a few minutes and I'll tell you."

Silence reigned in the office for over an hour. Danny scribbled furiously on a pad, while Omar did pushups and practiced handstands against the bookshelves. Sheet after sheet of paper was covered with half-completed grids, and Danny was beginning to claw his hair in frustration.

At half past one his torture came to an abrupt end. The office door opened and the curator walked in.

THIRTEEN

The curator of the Africa department jumped when he saw intruders in his office. Omar shrieked midhandstand and crumpled to the floor. Danny switched off the computer and started thinking up excuses.

"Who the Ra are you?" said the curator. "And what are you doing here?"

"We're from IT," said Danny quickly.

"We were testing your internet connection," said Omar.

"You weren't," said the curator. "You were testing your handstands."

Omar stifled a laugh. "Sorry, sir. They told us you'd gone to the Valley."

"The Valley of the Kings," said the curator, throwing his keys onto the desk. "Room 62. I'm in discussions with the Egyptology department about changes to the lighting on some of the mummies."

"That's what we thought, sir," said Omar, "but Mr. Chips said you'd gone to watch Charlton Athletic."

"Mr. Chips?"

"Our boss down at IT. When Mr. Chips heard 'the Valley,' he just assumed—"

"He shouldn't have assumed anything," snapped the curator. "He should have checked."

Danny glanced down at the magic square in front of him and a faint uneasiness stirred at the back of his mind. *I shouldn't have assumed anything. I should have checked.*

"You're right, sir," Omar was saying. "Our Mr. Chips is a few bytes short of a podcast, if you get my drift."

"Who is this Mr. Chips?" said the curator. "The head of IT is called Carruthers, not Chips."

Game over, thought Danny. *Go on, Grimps, get out of this one, if you can.*

Omar shuffled his feet nervously. "You mean you haven't heard the news?" he said.

"What news?" said the curator.

"About Carruthers."

"I haven't heard anything."

"I'm not sure whether I should tell you."

"Of course you should."

"Okay. Carruthers was leaving the museum late last night and got stopped by Bob from security. 'Could you show me your laptop bag, please?' says Bob, and Carruthers says, 'Why should I?' and Bob says, 'It's bulging' and Carruthers says, 'All right,' and he hands Bob the laptop bag. And what do you think Bob finds inside the laptop bag?"

"A laptop?"

"Not even a palmtop," whispered Omar, leaning toward the curator. "What Bob finds inside Carruthers's laptop bag is the Castellani Griffin Jug from Room 13."

"No!"

"Yes."

"That's terrible."

"Terrible for Carruthers," agreed Omar. "Good for Chips, though. Instant promotion. Sweet."

While Omar prattled on, Danny tidied the desk and concealed the evidence of his research. He tore his various scribblings off the top of the pad and stuffed them into his pockets. His mind was racing, full of new possibilities. *I shouldn't have assumed. I should have checked. The solution to the square has been staring me in the face!*

"Where do you think you're going?" asked the curator.

"We've got another job," said Danny.

"No," said the curator. "I'm not satisfied. Stay here, please, while I give your Mr. Chips a ring."

The curator picked up the phone and dialed. Omar edged toward the door.

"This is the Africa department," said the curator. "Give me Mr. Chips."

Omar caught Danny's eye and nodded slowly.

"Chips," repeated the curator. "C-H-I-P-S."

There was a short pause, and then the curator's face suddenly darkened. Danny and Omar lunged for the door.

"Stop!" cried the curator. "Carruthers, we have two intruders in the second-floor staff corridor. Sound the alarm!"

Danny and Omar rushed out into the corridor and sprinted along it toward the public galleries.

The double doors at the end of the corridor flew open and a shaven-headed guard appeared, scowling at the boys with fierce resolve. He wore a starched white shirt and a radio headset.

"Wall run!" cried Omar, putting on a burst of speed. As the two boys arrived where the guard stood, they swerved out of arm's reach, Danny left and Omar right. Up onto the wall— one, two, three paces—and a big dismount. They landed behind the guard and continued running, shoulder to shoulder.

The boys reached the double doors a moment before they clicked shut. Through the doors they ran and into the public gallery beyond. Gray-green carpets, light wood paneling, glass display cabinets. Swords, statues, calligraphic scrolls. Through another set of doors they ran and down a flight of steps. Skeleton in a basket. Golden chest. Mummified bull. Danny slowed to a walk, took off his parka, and turned it inside out. Omar stuffed his cap into the pocket of his tracksuit bottoms.

"How's your knee?" asked Danny.

"Good as new," said Omar. "Adrenaline is a great healer."

The Egyptian rooms were full of schoolchildren and tourists. Young and old were clustered around the mummies, murmuring, pointing, clicking. Danny and Omar slipped behind a large cabinet that held the massive outer cases of the mummies, huge sarcophagi of solid shining gold. The boys crouched down and caught their breath.

"You were good back there," whispered Danny. "You deserve a PHOM."

"What's that?"

"Physical Hacking Order of Merit."

"You did well too," said Omar.

"Me?" Danny unfolded the magic square and gazed down at it. "I'm as goofy as a griffin. I deserve to have my tiny brain sucked out through my nostrils like one of these mummies."

Omar chuckled and shook his head. "Don't worry, mate. That magic square's got no chance against the mighty Temple Brain."

"That's just it," whispered Danny. *"It's not a magic square!"*

"What?" Omar frowned. "But Redvald told us—"

"I know he did," said Danny. "He and I both made the same mistake. We added up the numbers in the first few rows and columns and they all made 175, so we just assumed that the whole square was magic. *We shouldn't have assumed. We should have checked.*"

"You think there's a row that doesn't add up?"

"One row and one column, to be exact," said Danny, gazing at the grid. *"One of the numbers is wrong."*

Three security guards entered the gallery from a side door

and pushed their way through the crowd toward Danny and Omar.

"Give me those Ritz matches of yours," said Danny.

Omar stared at him. "What?"

"Just do it!"

"Keep your hair on," said Omar. "Here you are."

Danny pulled the papers out of his pocket, lit a match, and held it to the corner of the treasure map. The papers curled and blackened as the flame spread.

"I hope you made copies of that," muttered Omar.

"No need," said Danny. *"I've solved it."*

Two schoolgirls noticed the smoke and began to scream. Danny kicked the flaming ball of paper into the corner and ran.

"Fire!" shouted someone. "Save the mummies!"

"Stuff the mummies!" cried another. "Let's get out of here!"

Danny and Omar joined a group of schoolchildren hurrying toward the exit. They ran across a footbridge and out onto the viewing platform of the Great Court. Huge porticos of flash-bulb marble glistened in the afternoon sun.

"Lift or stairs?" said Danny.

"Stairs."

Down the spiral staircase they ran, heading for the main exit, bounding four steps at a time, rubber soles squeaking on the polished marble. A lift pinged in an alcove down to their right. The doors opened and two guards stepped out into their path.

"Hold it right there."

Danny and Omar turned and ran back up the steps. But now there were footsteps in front of them as well, coming down fast.

"This way," said Omar, crane jumping onto the marble banister.

"That's not a way," panted Danny. "That's suicide."

Three meters away, right in the middle of the Great Court, stood an enormous Native American totem pole. Omar bent his knees and swung his arms.

"No!" cried Danny, but he was too late. Omar had already launched himself off the banister, arms windmilling like a long jumper's, feet stretched out before him in a bid for maximum distance. He landed on a massive bird beak halfway up the totem pole, clung to it for a moment, then loosened his grip and slid down. Danny watched his friend land softly on the marble floor of the Great Court and sprint through a doorway marked EMERGENCY EXIT ONLY.

Here goes. Danny sprang up onto the marble banister and measured the distance to the totem pole. *A traceur should know his limits. Explore your limits but never exceed them.*

"Don't even think about it, boyo," said a voice behind him. "I'm a bit squeamish, see, and I don't fancy scraping you off the floor of the Great Court—not now, not ever."

"I don't care if he tops himself," said another voice. "It's the exhibits I'm worried about. That half-witted friend of his nearly broke the beak off a priceless Nisga totem pole."

"If you jump and break the beak," said a third, "the chief of the Nisga will hunt you down and break *your* beak. Your call, though."

Danny knew in his heart that the jump was not going to work. He turned and hopped down onto the marble staircase. Strong hands grabbed his arms and held them fast.

"What's the matter, boyo?" snarled one of the guards. "Out of jump juice?"

FOURTEEN

Danny had watched enough television to have a pretty good grasp of police procedure, but this was his first time in a police station. The reception hall of the Agar Street Police Station smelled of disinfectant, and it was darker than he had expected.

"Empty your pockets," said the duty sergeant.

"Am I under arrest?" asked Danny.

"Not yet."

"Then you don't have the right to—"

"Empty your pockets!"

Danny did as he was told. Mobile phone. House keys. Penknife. Wallet.

"Nothing else?" The duty sergeant sounded disappointed.

"That's all."

"If we arrest you, we can have you searched properly."

"I know."

Danny was shown into an interview room and told to sit and

wait. There were no windows in the room, but there was a dark reflective panel on the wall opposite Danny. On the table in front of him was a tape recorder.

A middle-aged man in a shabby suit entered the room and sat down. "You are not yet under arrest," he said, "but I strongly advise you to cooperate." He pressed RECORD. "Monday, 25 October, ten past three in the afternoon, officer present Detective Inspector Carp. Please state your name for the tape."

"Daniel Oliver Temple."

"Age?"

"Sixteen."

"What were you doing at the British Museum?"

"Trying to get out."

"You were trespassing in the staff offices."

"We were lost."

"You tried to set fire to the mummies in Room 64."

"It was an accident."

"Of course." The detective popped a piece of nicotine gum into his mouth. "Lucky for you, the damage is superficial. Scorch marks on the floor."

"You don't think I've invoked the Curse of the Mummies, then?"

"No." Inspector Carp glanced down at his notebook. "But you seem to have invoked the Curse of the Redvald."

"Who?"

"Robin Redvald."

"Never heard of him."

"You split his lip."

"Has he filed a complaint?"

"Not yet." Detective Inspector Carp cracked his knuckles and leaned back in his chair.

"Then why am I here?" said Danny.

"For your own protection."

"How's that?"

The detective looked at his notes again. "The Knights of Akonio Dolo," he pronounced dramatically. "Ring any bells?"

"It's a Facebook group," said Danny. "Fifty psychos looking for some treasure."

"Fifty? You clearly haven't been online recently. The Knights of Akonio Dolo just cleared four hundred members, and one of the new knights is this Robin Redvald geezer you say you've never heard of. Redvald joined the treasure hunters at around midday, and the first thing he did was to post a fascinating account of a meeting he thinks he had with you. His story made everyone very excited, Daniel. There are hundreds of people out there who would dearly like to meet you."

Danny ran his tongue around the inside of his mouth. "Can't you just get Facebook to close down the group?"

"No chance. International law is a can of worms, Daniel, es-pecially when freedom of expression is at stake. The website is hosted in the Land of the Free, remember?"

"There must be *something* you can do."

Silence. Detective Inspector Carp glanced at the tape recorder and seemed to be wrestling with some strong impulse. Then his right index finger curled like the tail of a scorpion and jabbed the PAUSE button, making Danny jump.

Carp's eyes gleamed in his pockmarked face. "I can turn a blind eye to your activities in the British Museum today, and I can arrange protection for you until this is all over. But I need something concrete."

"Like what?"

"Like the map." Carp's voice was thick with greed. "Give me the map and I'll protect you from the evil hordes. I know people, Daniel. One hour from now, you could be off to Oz under a witness protection scheme."

"Oh really?"

"Really. Or you could be bleeding at the bottom of some lonely London stairwell. Your call."

Don't let him scare you. Danny bunched his fist and pressed his fingernails hard into the palm of his own hand.

"I burned the map," he said.

"Why?"

"I wanted to be rid of it."

The detective snorted loudly and popped more nicotine gum into his mouth. "If you don't start cooperating right now, Daniel Temple, I'll arrest you."

"Do," said Danny. "At least I get a lawyer that way."

"Is that so?"

"Yes." Danny tried to sound more confident than he was

feeling. "I know how the system works, Inspector Carp. You can either call me a lawyer or discharge me. In the meantime I'm not saying another word."

Carp stood up so violently that he knocked his chair over. "I know why you want to be arrested, you little prig. You're scared witless that those Dolo loonies are going to hunt you down. Well, they will, Daniel, starting the minute you leave here, and when they catch up with you, I won't be responsible for what they do."

At four forty-five in the afternoon, Danny was formally reprimanded for trespassing and discharged. The duty sergeant gave him back his belongings and Inspector Carp drove him back to Battersea in an unmarked police car, hurtling through the London traffic at sickening speed. By the time they were halfway to his flat, Danny's knuckles were bone white on the sides of the passenger seat.

"I can smell burning rubber," said Danny as they squealed round a traffic circle.

Inspector Carp did not slow down. "Tell me something, Daniel," he said. "How many of your Sunday school lessons do you remember?"

"A few. Why?"

"I was just thinking about your namesake, the prophet Daniel. Obstinate chappie, Daniel, always refusing to cooperate with the authorities. Until one day the authorities got tired of him and threw him into a den of lions. That's what's happening right now, isn't it, Daniel? The treasure hunters are out there, every one of them a hungry lion, and yet your stubbornness has left me with no choice: I have to throw you to them."

Carp screamed through a red light and swerved to miss a motorbike. Danny reached into his pocket and closed his fingers around his mobile phone.

"The way I remember it," said Danny, "the lions didn't so much as scratch him."

"Perhaps not." Carp unwrapped another piece of nicotine gum. "But when Daniel was on the edge of that pit with the guards about to shove him in, how sure was he that God would close the lions' mouths? More to the point, son, *how sure are you?*"

Danny knew his phone by touch and could send Omar a text without taking it out of his pocket: HELP. COME 2 BTRSEA.

"I almost forgot to tell you," continued Carp. "Your friend Bartholt has been cautioned and released."

"What!"

"Don't worry, though. He'd be mad to go after you again."

"But he *is* mad. They all are!"

"Mad as macaroons and ravenous as lions," said Carp. "Still, you've only yourself to blame. Here we are," he continued brightly, as the car screeched to a halt outside Danny's flat. "185 Battersea High Street. Or should I say Lion Lane?"

Danny turned in his seat to look up and down the street. It was already getting dark, and throngs of homeward-bound workers were hurrying along the sidewalk. A group of schoolboys loitered at the bus stop near the entrance to Danny's flat.

Smokers huddled in the doorway of the next-door pub. A little way down the street, a yellow-bearded tramp was engaged in earnest argument with a lamppost.

Danny felt a hand on his shoulder. "You're right on the edge of the lions' den, Daniel," whispered Carp, "but there's still a way back. *Just tell me where that gold is.*"

Danny shook off the hand and opened the car door.

"Four *hundred* knights," persisted Carp, "and they all know where you live. What makes you think you stand a chance up there?"

"I'm wearing my running shoes," said Danny, stepping out onto the sidewalk.

FIFTEEN

What *makes you think you stand a chance up there?* The question echoed in Danny's head as he tiptoed up the three flights of stairs to his apartment. The light in the stairwell was not working, so he had to feel the way in front of him with one hand. With his free hand he tried to phone Omar, but all he got was voicemail.

"Listen, Grimps," whispered Danny, "I'm at the flat to pick up some stuff. Come on over, yeah? Something's going to kick off—I can feel it. Oh, and call the Kinetix. We're going to need all the help we can get."

At the top of the stairs Danny's fingers touched a smooth metal door plaque: 185A, home sweet home. But this did not feel like a homecoming. *You're right on the edge of the lions' den, Daniel.*

Danny entered, locked the door behind him, and took several deep breaths to calm himself. On the third breath he noticed the sour smell of body odor. Somebody unsavory was already here. Danny's first impulse was to run, but he stopped himself. *Passport first, and then escape.*

The intruder was sitting on the far side of the room, his face lit eerily from below by the blue-white glow of a laptop screen. Danny recognized him as one of the Americans from HOPE, the cocky one who had hacked Whitehall. And he still had egg in his hair. *What was his name again? Isembard Cornell.*

"Yo," said the intruder.

"Don't yo me," said Danny, flicking on the lights. "What are you doing here?"

"Cool it, stress puppy."

"You're in my flat!"

"Yadda yadda, who's been eating *my* porridge? Spare me the Three Bears, dude. I've had a lame weekend, and the last thing I need is you breaking my crayons."

"You're one of Them, aren't you?" said Danny.

Isembard laughed. "Them with a capital T, Danny? How deliciously *tribal* that sounds."

"That's my laptop you're using."

"It's called hot-desking."

"It's called trespassing. I should know—I've just been busted for it."

Danny looked up at the skylight he had boarded up only last night. The board was gone. Nothing up there now except the inky night sky.

"Fix me a sandwich," said Isembard. "I haven't eaten since yesterday."

"Fix it yourself," snapped Danny. "You seem to know where everything is." He went to the bookshelf and took down *A Dummy's Guide to UNIX*. The middle pages had been hollowed out to make a secret hiding place for his passport and money.

Danny turned his back on Isembard and put the money in his wallet. He slipped the wallet and passport into the pockets of his tracksuit bottoms and ticked off a mental checklist: passport, wallet, phone, keys, penknife. He was ready. All he cared about now was the journey ahead of him.

"What are you doing, dude?" drawled Isembard.

"None of your business," said Danny, heading for the door. "I liked your conference talk, by the way. Shame about the egg."

The American slammed the laptop shut and jumped to his feet. "How did you get in?" he said.

"It's my flipping flat," replied Danny. "How did *you* get in?"

The hacker snorted. "I'm talking Timbuktu, dude. What was your way in?"

Danny paused with his hand on the front door latch and turned to face his rival. "Skype tunnels," he said. "I installed a plug-in on the Timbuktu side and turned it into a zombie. I take it the knights bagged you as well."

"Harrrrr." Isembard winked theatrically and curled his right hand into a hook. "Right you are, Jim lad. Bagged on Bag-a-Hacker Day, and forced to code all night."

"How did it go?" Danny knew he should be leaving, but he was interested in spite of himself. "Did you manage to hack Timbuktu?"

"Timbuk-too flipping late," said Isembard. "I finally got access at seven this morning, only to find that someone had been there six minutes before me and run a full delete."

"That was me," said Danny.

"You peed on my barbecue, dude. Six freaking minutes!"

"Sorry."

The American gave a strange lopsided smile. "You will be."

"That's a threat, is it?" said Danny. "What is it with black-hats and revenge? I beat you to Timbuktu fair and square."

"I don't want revenge, you histrionic twerp. I want the map! I came here to look for traces of it on your hard drive."

"You won't find anything."

"I know that now. That's why we've been waiting for you."

"We?" Danny tried not to let the fear show in his voice.

"We knights," drawled Isembard. "Like you say, I'm one of Them now."

"Where are the others?"

"All around us, dude. In the street, on the roof, on the stairs, and right here in the apartment. I'm just the front man, see? Think of me as the receptionist."

As if on cue, somebody somewhere began to sing. The voice was deep and husky, and it took a moment for Danny to realize where it was coming from.

> "Oh Danny boy, the pipes, the pipes are calling
> From glen to glen, and down the mountain side.

The summer's gone and all the roses falling—
'Tis you, 'tis you must go and I must bide."

The voice was coming from under Danny's bed. And others were joining in one by one—from the wardrobe, the bathroom, the stairwell, the landing. Danny started to shake. He had heard the song many times before but never had it sounded so menacing.

"Shiver your timbers!" cried Isembard Cornell. "How's *that* for surround sound?"

Danny did not hear. He was staring transfixed at the skylight. Two men in black balaclavas were standing on the roof looking down at him, singing their hearts out.

"Let me explain how this is going to work," Isembard was saying. "You and me and the knights are going to sit down together and have a time of sharing. First slot is yours, of course, and your theme will be the magic square of Akonio Dolo and its solution. Do you think you'll be needing PowerPoint?"

"Leave me alone," said Danny.

The wardrobe door swung open and a man in a purple balaclava stepped out into the room. Another was wriggling out feet first from under the bed. *Grimps,* breathed Danny, *what would* you *do?*

"Be of good courage, Baby Bear," drawled Isembard Cornell. "Tell us what you know and maybe we'll fix you some porridge for dinner."

Danny crouched down, put his hands together, and closed his eyes.

"Oh *please*," said the American. "That won't save you. I've never seen anyone so *totally trapped*."

"A traceur," said Danny quietly, "is never trapped." He jumped high into the air, knees tucked up to his chest, eyes still tightly shut. As he landed, his hand shot up to the light switch and the whole room went dark.

There was a moment of stunned silence, broken by a shout of rage from over by the wardrobe. "Get him!"

Danny had two advantages over his adversaries. He knew the layout of the room better than they did, and by shutting his eyes he had already adjusted them to the darkness. He had a head start and intended to make the most of it.

Parkour is not so very different from hacking. Traceur and hacker both require special techniques, special vision. Both move freely to surpass the barriers erected by man to enclose and restrict. Parkour and hacking are about one thing only: freedom.

Danny saw the American hacker blundering toward him in the darkness, so he ducked down and rolled out of the way. Keeping low, he scampered across the floor in a wide curve, making for the electric heater.

Parkour vision is an illness—la maladie du traceur. *When you parkour, you see things differently. You see alternative paths to your objective, and the longer you practice, the more paths you see.*

"Don't let him escape!" cried a voice from the wardrobe.

"Someone turn the lights on!" yelled another.

"It's all right," said a third voice. "I've got him."

"No, you oaf! That's *me!*"

Someone found the lights and switched them on. The hooded men blinked rapidly and gazed around them. Danny Temple was nowhere to be seen. He was not in the kitchen or the bathroom or the wardrobe. He was not on the landing either. It was as if he had evaporated.

"Check the windows!" bellowed the man in the purple balaclava.

"All locked."

"Skylight!"

"Nope," came a voice from the roof. "We were right here the whole time."

Purple Balaclava turned to Isembard Cornell, eyes bulging with rage. "You useless code monkey!" he yelled. "That's the last time you front a knights mission."

Cornell raked a hand through his hair, scattering dried egg all around him. "Call me unromantic," he said, "but what's with the male voice choir? I don't remember that being part of the plan."

Another of the knights was staring at the electric heater. "Quit blamestorming and check this out," he said. "It's been moved."

He was right. The heater now stood almost eighteen inches from the wall, revealing an old Victorian fireplace behind.

"There's a chimney!" shouted Purple Balaclava. "The little tyke's gone up the chimney!"

"Nice," mouthed Isembard Cornell.

"Ronnie, PJ! Get away from that skylight and look for where the chimney comes out. Can you see him?"

"Flip, yes! He's on the roof!"

Urban monkey. Traceur extraordinaire. *Master of all I survey. I stand on the roofs of Battersea High Street, and before me stretches half a mile of concrete, walls, rails, and chimneys. Chelsea Harbor down to my left, London Eye away to my right. How many days have I run this roof, and in how many different ways? How many nights has my dream self flowed across the city skyline, swan dived over steeples, cat jumped from one skyscraper to the next?*

Danny jumped off the chimney stack, rolled on the concrete roof, got up, and ran for his life.

SIXTEEN

The moon sat low in the sky, peeking between the girders of the great wheel called the London Eye like a sleep-
less toddler through banisters. Danny was wide awake as
well. *There's nothing like pursuit to focus the mind.*

Softly over the roofs he sped, and behind him ran the knights.
Stay focused, thought Danny. *The knights may be fast but they're
unskilled. They're no match for a practiced traceur. Just concentrate
and watch your technique.*

Up here the darkness was as good as light because Danny
knew these roofs by heart. He knew there were ten strides between this obstacle and that, eleven to the next, ten, ten, fourteen, ten, thirteen, ten, and then five to the fire escape. *Kong,
kong, underpass, swan. Double kong, underpass, kash vault, kong.
Flow like water over your course. Watch and weep, gravity slaves.*

He did not turn round, but the sound effects behind him
told a story of botched pursuit: the scuff and slap of novice on
concrete, the bumble and stumble of blind vaulting, the pained

curses of the inept. It was a shame Omar was not here to see this. He'd have laughed his head off.

Four more sections of roof and then the dismount. Once he was on the edge of the roof, he'd be all set. He would climb halfway down the fire escape and then perform his YouTube party piece, a stunning dismount involving three consecutive 180-degree cat passes: fire escape, balcony, trash container, ground. Twist, twist, twist, roulade, thank you very much.

But Danny did not get as far as the end of the roof. He clipped his feet on an easy kong vault four sections from the end, flung out an arm to protect his head, and rolled awkwardly, bruising his shoulder and tailbone on the concrete. He stuck out a hand and felt a twinge in his wrist.

"PJ, did you hear that?" The voice came from not far away. "Chimpanzee boy's fallen over."

Danny sat up and groaned. His left wrist was agony. *You deserve it for thinking too far ahead,* he said to himself. *How many times has Omar lectured you about staying in the moment? Lose concentration midkong and you trail a foot. Trail a foot, bail the vault. Bail the vault, break your face. You're a prat, Danny.*

Raising his head above the level of the wall, Danny saw three of his pursuers silhouetted against a patch of moonlit sky. They were vaulting better now, and in a few seconds they would be on top of him.

"Is he hurt?"

"I think so. Too cocky for his own good, that one."

Danny cradled his wrist and winced. It was time to reconsider the escape route. This wrist wouldn't be any good for climbing down fire escapes, let alone absorbing the shock of three consecutive cat passes. He needed another plan.

An idea came to him. He dismissed it. It came back. He dismissed it again. It was a splendidly half-baked idea, the sort of idea that earns you posthumous awards and a mention in *Bizarre* magazine. But it was the only idea he had. He wet his finger and held it up. *Good. At least the wind is right.*

Danny pulled off his tracksuit bottoms and scrunched them up in his right hand. Then he hopped up onto the low dividing wall to face his pursuers. *Come on, knights. Let's play chess.* A sudden weird elation made Danny break into a little dance right there on the wall.

The Knights of Akonio Dolo stopped. A band of fox hunters would have been no less surprised to turn a corner and find their fox tap-dancing along the top of a fence.

"I found myself some Dogon gold in the Dounagouna pass," chanted Danny. "I girded my loins and took the coins and hid them—"

"*Get him!*" The hooded knights surged forward, arms outstretched to seize their prey. Danny hopped off the wall and sprinted the last three sections of roof in ten seconds flat. Thirteen paces and a kong vault, ten paces and a turn vault, five paces and a *LEAP* into the void!

In moments of extreme stress, human beings are capable of great courage, strength, and creativity. Adrenaline, the enemy of rational thought, is also a worker of miracles. On countless occasions Danny had stood on that roof and looked down at the river beyond the South Bank path, imagining the same thing every time: How would it feel to leap off this roof into the river?

Now he knew. It was sickening.

It was like the momentary plummeting sensation Danny sometimes experienced on the edge of sleep, except protracted into three horrible bottomless seconds. Three seconds, three stories, three images before his eyes. *Omar Dupont, Galileo Galilei, Akonio Dolo*. He saw Omar launching off the marble staircase in the British Museum. He saw Galileo dropping a cannonball off the leaning tower of Pisa. And last of all he saw Akonio Dolo jumping off a mud-brick minaret to certain death. *Acceleration due to gravity: 9.8 meters per second every second.*

As he accelerated toward the river, Danny turned himself head down. He held his nose with his left hand and with his good arm he flung his tracksuit bottoms as hard as he could toward the South Bank path. *The passport and cash must not get wet.*

Splash! He sliced the water hand head chest legs feet and continued down into the silty depths of the river, dizzy with relief and shock. The pain in his wrist was excruciating, but he welcomed it as evidence of life. He had done it. He was the only member of the Kinetix to have jumped off a three-story building into the River Thames.

Danny resurfaced and hauled himself up onto dry ground, shocked at how close to the concrete edge he had splashed down. Half a meter less and he would have been spread all over the South Bank path. They would have had to identify him from dental records. Drenched to the skin, he lurched forward onto the path.

"Danny! Is that you?"

Danny dropped into a crouch, the hairs standing up on the back of his neck. Then recognition came.

"Grimps!" he shouted. "I'm over here!"

The two boys stumbled toward each other, triggering a security light on the wall of the riverside flats.

"There you are," said Danny. "You took your time."

"Look up!" cried Omar. Was it just the glare of the light, or was Omar's face as white as a sheet?

Danny looked up and saw half a dozen knights sprinting down the fire escape, taking the steps several at a time. The front-runners were already nearing the ground.

"I've got a few of them on my tail as well," said Omar. "Let's split!"

"Wait!" Danny looked around for his tracksuit bottoms. "I need to get my stuff."

"Forget your stuff!"

"No!" Danny cast around wildly. "I need my passport! That's the reason I went back."

The tracksuit bottoms lay crumpled on the grass nearby. Danny tried to pull them on over his wet running shoes, but his wrist was hurting too much.

"Leave them, Danny!" It was not like Omar to sound so scared. "I said leave them!"

"Okay, fine!" Danny took his things out of the pockets—

passport, wallet, phone, keys, penknife—and gave them to Omar. He would just have to run trouserless for a while.

Omar shoved Danny's things into his backpack and sprinted away up the South Bank path. Danny followed, his long-sleeved top clinging wetly to his body and his running shoes squelching with every step.

The man in the purple balaclava was first off the fire escape. He took the last flight of steps in one enormous leap and hit the ground running, pounding up the South Bank path in hot pursuit. His style was noisy, flat-footed, and remarkably fast.

"What's the plan?" said Danny. "Did you call the Kinetix like I asked?"

"They're on their way," said Omar. "We're meeting at six o'clock at Clapham Junction. Now shut up and concentrate on your parkour."

Omar jumped onto a bench, vaulted some high iron railings, landed in a back garden, and rolled. Danny followed, vaulting to the right so as not to put weight on his bad wrist.

Shoulder to shoulder Danny and Omar ran. They jumped a flower bed, konged a fence, and tic-tac-ed onto the roof of a rabbit hutch. *Kash vault, cat pass, dive kong, lache. Bunny rabbits, toolshed, garages, lawn. Ouch, ouch, ouch.*

"No more vaults," gasped Danny. "My wrist is killing me."

"Oi!" Someone was shouting from an upstairs window. "Get out of my garden or I'm calling the police!"

The boys swung themselves up into the fork of an apple tree, climbed out on a limb, and dismounted into the next garden.

They ran across three more gardens, jumping the fences in between and triggering one security light after another.

"There's a clothesline," said Danny. "At least let me grab some pants!"

"No time!" cried Omar, and something in his voice made Danny believe him. *What had happened to Omar to rattle him like this?*

Purple Balaclava was still close behind them. He was moving fast for a big man but was certainly no traceur. Parkour demands stealth; this man was charging along like an angry rhinoceros.

The fifth garden in the row might have been the result of a TV makeover. It featured lots of decking, a fountain, and hardly any plants.

"You claustrophobic?" asked Omar.

"No," said Danny.

"You will be soon."

Omar threw himself face-down on the ground and wriggled underneath the decking. Danny followed suit. The wooden planks were no more than eight inches off the ground, so he had to press his whole body against the earth, coating his bare legs in mud. Danny cared less about the dirt than about the pain. A flat cat crawl is difficult at the best of times, but with a sprained wrist it was a nightmare.

"No farther," panted Danny. "My whole arm's on fire here."

"Can't stop now," said Omar. "We've got a bus to catch."

Blind as moles, they wriggled around the side of the house and squirmed out into the open.

"Sloane Street," said Danny.

"And there's the Clapham Junction bus," said Omar, hopping over the low wall onto the sidewalk. Sure enough, a red double-decker bus was hurtling into view. The driver ignored Omar's outstretched arm and sped up the road toward the bus stop. Danny and Omar ran after it, yelling and waving.

"We're too late," said Danny.

"Not necessarily. Look."

The bus had stopped, and there were a dozen people waiting to get on. Each person was worth one or two precious seconds.

The boys made it by a whisker, nipping onto the bus just before it closed its doors. While Omar was swiping his fare card, Danny glanced back down the road, and to his horror he saw Purple Balaclava dart out of a side street and race toward the bus.

The driver had a large bald head and a wisp of side-combed hair. He was staring stonily at Danny.

"Sorry, lad," he said. "You can't travel half naked on a London bus. It's indecent."

"I'm wearing shorts," said Danny.

"Hardly," snorted the driver. "You're wearing boxer shorts."

"He's a boxer," interrupted Omar. "Don't make him prove it."

"I don't give a monkey's if he's Ahmed blinking Khan!" said the driver. "He's filthy and he's stinking and he's got no trousers on." The driver pulled a lever and the doors swung open. "Read my lips, sonny boy: We aren't going anywhere until Dirty Knees gets off."

Danny glanced in the offside wing mirror and saw that their pursuer was getting close. As Danny watched, he whipped off his balaclava to reveal an unshaven face and a tousle of lank curls. *Bartholt.* The words printed at the bottom of the wing mirror added to Danny's unease: *Objects in the mirror are closer than they appear.*

"You can't do this," said Omar to the driver. "My friend has already paid for his journey."

"How's that, then?"

"I swiped his fare card for him."

"That wasn't his card, it was yours."

"I wish," Omar replied, chuckling and handing over a ten-pound note. "I'm paying in cash, me."

"But I thought—"

"Tell you what." Omar lowered his voice. "Let my friend travel and you can keep the change."

"I don't know."

"Go on. You're already late as it is."

The word *late* had an immediate effect. The driver closed the doors and pulled away from the curb with a loud sigh. At that moment, Bartholt came running up alongside, banging on the doors of the bus. "Open up!" he yelled. "Let me on!"

"Blasted yob," muttered the bus driver, changing into second gear. "He's going to smash something if he carries on like that."

"Temple!" yelled Bartholt, banging on the window nearest Danny. "You're toast, Temple."

Danny and Omar climbed the steps to the top deck of the bus and went all the way to the back, where people wouldn't stare so much.

"He's given up," whispered Omar. "He's just standing there fiddling with his phone."

"Not fiddling," said Danny. "Updating his Facebook group and spreading the word to all his barmy friends. *Targets are traveling on a Number 145 bus, heading toward Clapham Junction train station.*"

"*Zut,*" said Omar. "As I always say, a traceur is never trapped *except* on a London bus. Not exactly much room for maneuver, is there?"

The two boys plunked themselves down on the back seats, utterly exhausted. Danny was cradling his aching wrist.

"I can't believe you did the river jump," said Omar. "That was the coolest thing I've ever seen."

"Thanks."

"And the stupidest. Without the following wind you would have ended up I Can't Believe It's Not Butter-ed all over the South Bank path."

"I knew the jump would work," said Danny. "I did the math."

Omar stared out of the window and clenched his fists as if trying to exorcise some terrible memory.

"Cough it up," said Danny. "What happened to you after we got split up at the British Museum?"

"I got lucky at first," said Omar. "I found a rubbish truck at the back of the museum canteen and hopped into the crusher just before it drove off. Sailed right through security and got out in Montague Place."

"That was a risk."

"Life's a risk. I went back to my dorm at school—thought it would be quiet, being half-term and all, but a bunch of the guys were waiting for me there. You know how fast news travels on Facebook. They kept asking about you and the map and Timbuktu. You remember Rees and Angus, don't you?"

"What have they done now?"

"They've only gone and joined the Knights of Akonio Dolo. They made these stupid *KOAD* buttons for themselves."

"Did they hassle you?"

"They dragged me into the WC and flushed me. Wanted me to tell them where the treasure is."

"You don't know where it is."

"That's what I told them."

"They didn't buy it?"

"Course not."

"But you got away."

"Eventually." Omar scowled. "And since then I've been running nonstop. I'm like that stupid bird, what's-his-name?"

"Orville?"

"Road Runner. It's like I escape from one knight and run smack into another."

"What you need is a break."

"Tell me about it."

"You've got your passport?"

"Yes."

"Come to Africa with me."

Omar's jaw dropped. "You're off your nut!"

"Think about it," said Danny. "Our lives in London are over. You couldn't go back to school even if you wanted to, and I certainly can't go back to my flat. Bartholt was right—I'm toast. And unless you hand me over to the knights pretty quick, so are you."

Omar nodded slowly. "I suppose we could go to France and stay with my parents for a bit," he said. "But I'm not going to Africa. There's no point."

"I can think of two million points," said Danny. "*I've solved the square, Grimps.* We'd never forgive ourselves if we didn't go out there and have a gander."

"It's flipping *Africa*," hissed Omar. "We don't know anyone in Africa."

"And no one knows us," said Danny. "Which means we don't get chased or interrogated or flushed."

"I'll tell you this, mate, I'd rather be flushed than boiled in a cauldron."

"Get a grip," said Danny. "Africa isn't all doom and gloom and head-hunting cannibals, you know. You've been reading too many Tintin comics."

Omar glared out the window in silence and then shook his head again. "It's not going to happen," he said. "How are we going to buy food there when we don't even speak the language?"

"You do speak the language," said Danny. "The national language of Mali is French."

"Zut."

SEVENTEEN

Danny and Omar got off the bus at the last stop before Clapham Junction station and ducked into the doorway of a sports shop.

"Closed," said Omar, peering through the door into the dark interior. "No pants for you, bro, unless we smash a window."

"Leave it," said Danny. "There's a Red Cross charity shop in Grant Road, right behind the train station."

"That'll be shut, too."

"Yes, but think about it. Say you went to a charity shop with stuff to donate and you found the shop shut, what would you do?"

"I'd dump the stuff in the doorway and go home."

"Correct," said Danny. "You're a lazy dog, and you wouldn't be the only one. There must be clothes sitting outside that shop right now, just waiting for the trouserless."

The boys sprinted up the sidewalk, turned into Grant Road, and ran past a row of shop fronts. Butcher, baker, joystick maker,

Red Lion, Red Cross, William Hill. The Red Cross shop was dark and lifeless, but sure enough there were already a couple of large plastic bags in the doorway. Danny and Omar kneeled down and began to search the bags.

"Them's mine," slurred a voice behind them. "Scram. I saw 'em first."

Danny turned and saw the familiar outlines of beard and bottle, silhouetted against the glow of a streetlight. *Oh no. This is all we need.*

"Chill," said Omar to the tramp. "There's plenty to go around. Look, here's an I LOVE LONDON mug."

The vagrant took the mug and emptied his bottle into it. "I lub Lurdon," he said.

Danny went on searching the bags, but there was nothing suitable in either of them. The only clothes here were old men's clothes: corduroy trousers, bad ties, overcoats, and a brown felt hat.

"Give us a look!" shouted the tramp. "I was 'ere first!"

"All right," said Omar, handing him the hat. "Have a hat."

"Bless you," said the tramp, and he put it on his head.

Danny turned to Omar. "This is all wrong," he said. "Why am I looking for streetwear?"

"Streetwear's what we wear."

"Yes, but it's just what the knights will be expecting: a sixteen-year-old wearing a cap, a jacket, and tracksuit bottoms. If I walk into Clapham Junction wearing street, I might as well wear an AKONIO DOLO sandwich board too." He tore off his wet shirt and chose a dry one from the bag. Then he pulled on the corduroy trousers, overcoat, socks, and brown shoes. "You should get a disguise as well, Grimps."

"No way. I'd rather be flushed than wear that stuff."

"Suit yourself." Danny turned to the tramp. "Give me back my hat."

"What 'at?"

"That one." Danny grabbed the hat and put it on his head.

The tramp looked stunned for a moment and then flung out a hamlike fist in the direction of Danny's nose. Danny ducked, swerved out of arm's reach, and began to run.

"'E filched me 'at!" yelled the tramp. "Call the cops! Call Scotland Lard! Feral youths at the chattery shop!"

Danny and Omar sprinted toward the station. It was all Danny could do to stay upright in his new shoes; they were too big and had hardly any grip. "Where are we meeting the Kinetix?" he panted.

"Main entrance," said Omar. "Less chance of being spotted."

The boys joined the steady stream of people entering the station. Clapham Junction was the busiest train station in Europe, and this was rush hour, so a magnificent herd of human beings was tramping in and out of the station through the St. John's Hill shopping center.

"Keep your head down, Grimps," whispered Danny. "This place is probably crawling with knights."

"Stop trying to freak me out."

"You there," said a voice at Danny's side. "Step this way, please."

The speaker wore a yellow plastic jacket and carried a walkie-talkie. *It's one of them* was Danny's first thought. *No it's not* was his second thought. *It's Baz.*

Baz Dervish, the leader of the Kinetix, was twenty years old. He was short for his age, but he had been doing parkour a long time and commanded massive respect among the gang. Baz had a shaved head, an eyebrow piercing, and the highest jump of any of them, a colossal flying leap that had to be seen to be believed. Earlier that year he had PK-ed in a TV commercial for Elito running shoes. He was one of Danny's heroes.

Danny and Omar followed their leader to the doorway of a flower shop. "Nice disguise," whispered Danny.

"Cheers," said Baz. "It's funny the way a bright yellow jacket and a walkie-talkie make you completely invisible. Anyway, what's the plan? Are we your bodyguards?"

"Something like that," said Danny. "Just watch out for knights and try to keep them off our tail."

"Which train are you catching?"

"Gatwick Airport." Danny glanced up at the departure board. "It leaves from Platform 13 exactly seven and a half minutes from now."

"How do we recognize knights?" asked Baz.

"You can tell them by their horses," volunteered Omar, "and occasionally by their shining armor."

"Shut up, Grimps," said Danny. "There's only one way to spot them, so far as I can see. Real commuters don't show much interest in other people, but these knights will be looking around a lot, studying the faces in the crowd."

Baz dropped to one knee and raised the walkie-talkie to his mouth. "This is Beta," he said. "I'm in the concourse with Delta and Omega. They need Platform 13. Our job is to see them safely onto their train and take out any opposition. Over."

The walkie-talkie crackled faintly and a voice came through. "This is Ash. What do you mean, 'take out'? Over."

"Use your imagination, over," Baz snapped, then glanced up at Danny and Omar. "You boys still here? I thought you had a train to catch."

"Thanks," said Danny. "We owe you one."

"Go!"

Danny and Omar mingled with the crowd. Danny turned up his collar and pulled the brim of his hat all the way down over his eyebrows.

The woman at the ticket window had worry lines across her forehead and dark shadows under her eyes. She hardly looked at Danny as he asked for two one-way tickets to Gatwick and handed over a twenty-pound note.

Through the ticket barrier they went and along the brightly lit passage, shuffling toe-to-heel with a thousand other commuters. On either side of the passage, flights of steps led up to the platforms. A loud rumble and a rush of hydraulic brakes told Danny that a train was arriving overhead at Platform 8.

Omar stiffened suddenly. "Blue parka at eleven o'clock," he whispered. "Is that who I think it is?"

Danny raised his eyes and scanned the crowd. A legion of white collars was marching toward them, and among them was one blue parka. The face above the parka was indeed familiar: thin nose, arched eyebrows, hollow cheeks. It was Robin Redvald.

That meeting in the SOAS roof garden—had it really only happened this morning? It seemed long ago. Danny remembered the windmills, the larvikite, and the scent of lemon thyme. *Where did you get this? You've got a nerve, bringing this here.* Accusation, denial, elbow, blood, it had all happened so fast. And now the historian had turned knight. *You seem to have invoked the Curse of the Redvald, Danny.*

Robin Redvald passed close to Danny and walked on without even breaking his stride. The disguise had worked! Or had it? Danny glanced back and saw to his horror that Redvald had stopped. He was standing stock-still and the crowd flowed around him like a babbling brook around a stone. *Don't turn around, Redvald. Don't turn around.*

Redvald did not turn around. He shook his head slightly and went on walking toward the ticket barriers. The boys watched the tiny bald spot on the back of Redvald's head as it bobbed away down the tunnel.

"Phew," said Danny. "I thought he'd clocked us."

"Nah, we're fine," said Omar. "He was just enjoying a little Zen moment, that's all."

How wrong they were.

EIGHTEEN

Robin Redvald reached the ticket barriers but did not go through. Instead he turned left into a little newspaper stall and speed dialed a number on his phone.

"I just saw them," he said. "They're walking east-west toward Platforms 10 to 17. Temple has changed into an overcoat and a brown felt hat. Dupont is still wearing his tracksuit and orange baseball cap. Tell the others."

The historian took off his parka, stuffed it in his briefcase, and headed back up the passage toward the platforms. He had lost sight of Temple and Dupont for the time being, but that was unimportant. What mattered was that the boys' cover was well and truly blown.

Redvald stopped at a tacky souvenir stall to buy a baseball cap, then hurried on. *Board a train, monkey boys, any train. Bartholt has got five knights on every platform, each of them itching to bag you. No amount of running and jumping can save you this time.*

A sudden bong from the loudspeaker heralded a passenger

announcement. "The next train to arrive at Platform 12 is the eighteen fifteen South West Trains service for Dorking, calling at Earlsfield, Wimbledon, Raynes Park, Worcester Park, Stoneleigh, Epsom, Ashstead, Leatherhead, and Dorking."

Worth a look, thought Redvald. He turned left and jogged up the steps onto Platform 12. A crush of men and women lined the platform, craning their necks and jostling politely for position. There were plenty of caps and ladies' hats in the crowd, but not a single brown felt hat.

"Hey! Over here! Somebody help me!" The voice was coming from farther along the platform, near the MEN sign.

Redvald ventured into the men's room.

"Help!" The voice was louder now and seemed to be coming from one of the stalls. Redvald pushed open the door and saw a spiky-haired teenager handcuffed to the U bend of the toilet.

"What do you do?" asked Redvald.

"Detecting, dowsing, digging, diving, whatever it takes," answered the boy, giving the correct password.

"Who did this to you?"

"No idea. I'm on the platform and I see this lad in a hat, and his mate's got a cap, and I think to myself, *That's Temple.* So I'm walking up behind them when suddenly these two nutters in black tracksuits come flying out of nowhere, leap on top of me, and drag me in here."

Redvald speed dialed. "We've got a problem, Bartholt. Temple and Dupont are not working alone. They've got friends."

"How many?"

"At least two."

"Diddums. Is Christopher Robin frightened? Does he want to go home to Pooh? *Get a grip, Christopher Robin!* We've got *eighty-five* men in the station and more arriving by the second. Now get off the phone!"

"Don't call me Christopher Robin," said Robin Redvald, but Bartholt had already rung off.

How dare he accuse me of being frightened? thought Redvald. He hated working with this Bartholt man, but he saw no other way. After all, he told himself, *your enemy's enemy is your friend.*

Another bong from the PA system made Redvald jump. "The train now approaching Platform 12 is the eighteen fifteen South West Trains service for Dorking, calling at Earlsfield, Wimbledon, Raynes Park, Worcester Park . . ."

The historian headed out onto the platform, ignoring the cries of the handcuffed knight. A train was arriving, which meant there was serious people watching to be done. He hopped up onto a luggage cart where he could get a good view along the whole length of the train.

The 18:15 hissed to a halt and doors slid open. People got off. People got on. There was no sign of Temple or Dupont anywhere.

"The train now standing at Platform 12 is the eighteen fifteen South West Trains service for Dorking. Please mind the gap between the train and the platform edge."

Redvald tried to concentrate on the crowd, but he was feeling a peculiar prickling sensation on the back of his neck. There was no denying it: The testimony of the handcuffed knight had unnerved him. *These two nutters in black tracksuits come flying out of nowhere, leap on top of me, and drag me in here.* Robin Redvald was not a brave man and he hated the sound of those avenging angels. *Quis spectat spectatores,* he wondered. *Who is watching the watchers?*

An assortment of stragglers was sprinting up the passage steps, hoping to board the train before the doors closed. Redvald jumped off the luggage cart and hurried down the platform, scrutinizing the latecomers as they hurled themselves onto the train. But none of these blurs of newspaper and coattails was Danny Temple.

"Please mind the gap," droned the loudspeaker, and the train doors beeped urgently.

Out of the corner of his eye, the historian saw a small figure dart out from the shadow of a coffee vending machine. *A small figure in a brown felt hat.* Redvald stuck out a foot and the figure sprawled on the platform.

"Knights of Akonio Dolo!" yelled Redvald. "Bag him!"

But Danny Temple was not hanging around to be bagged. He grabbed his hat, rolled to his right, and slithered down through the gap between the train and the platform edge.

"Hold the train!" screamed Redvald. "There's someone on the track!"

"Man on the line!" cried a station guard farther up the platform. "Hold the train!"

Redvald looked around and saw two men in black tracksuits

bearing down on him. *So this is what avenging angels look like.* Surprisingly, the history student was no longer afraid. He was furious. This was the second time that monkey boy had eluded him, and he was determined that it would not happen again. Shaking with anger, Redvald flung down his briefcase and plunged into the gap between the train and the platform edge.

"Two men on the line!" The guard's voice sounded distant and indistinct, like a voice from another world. "Call the transport police!"

There was not much light beneath the train, but Redvald spotted his prey immediately. The boy seemed to be heading toward the link between cars, where there was enough space to crawl across to the opposite platform.

"Temple!" Redvald bellowed, crawling after him. "Stay right where you are!"

"Is that you, Redvald?" The boy's voice was tight, as if trying to hide his fear. "I hear you're a knight now. What made you go over to the dark side?"

"Listen, Temple. That is a live line! Don't move a muscle!"

"Sorry, mate. Moving's what I do."

"You're going to fry yourself! Just stay there, do you hear? I'm coming to get you."

Redvald smiled to himself in the darkness. *I'm coming to get you.* That part at least was true. But he had lied about the rails being live. At main-line stations the trains got their power from overhead wires, as any train spotter would know.

The boy started moving much more slowly, trying to pick

his way through that strange and terrible underworld without touching the rails. *Clearly Danny Temple is no train spotter.* Redvald scrambled after him in an ungainly cat crawl, touching the rails willy-nilly as he neared his prey. Before the boy could reach the far side of the train, Redvald stretched out a hand and caught him by the left foot.

"Get off!" cried Danny, trying to kick free.

"On one condition," said the historian. "You come back to SOAS with me and talk to my professors."

"No."

"They want to meet you."

"Tough."

"Think of Professor Wiseman at the Timbuktu Manuscripts Project. Don't you think he has a right to know what was stolen from him?"

"No."

"I'm not saying *you* stole it, Danny, but it came into your hands all the same, and it's wrong to hang on to something that isn't yours."

"In that case," said Danny, "kindly *let go of my foot!*" He kicked hard, and his left shoe came off in the historian's hand.

Danny Temple slithered out from under the train, ran across the tracks, and muscled up onto the far platform. A tall red-haired boy was running toward him, but Danny evaded him with a neat sidestep and plunged on into the waiting room.

"The train now approaching Platform 13 is the eighteen seventeen Southern Trains service to Brighton. Calling at East

Croydon, Gatwick Airport, Three Bridges, Wivelsfield, Hassocks, Preston Park, and Brighton."

Redvald hobbled across the track in front of the approaching train and was helped up onto Platform 13 by two men in blue jumpsuits.

"What do you two do?" Redvald asked.

"Detecting, dowsing, digging, diving," they chanted in unison, "whatever it takes."

"Temple went into that waiting room," said Redvald, pointing. "How many doors does it have?"

"Just the one."

"Tickety-boo," said the historian. "We've got him. Text Bartholt and tell him to send everyone over here right now."

While the treasure hunters fumbled with their phones, Redvald gazed at the closed door marked WAITING ROOM. *You're a slippery one, Danny Temple, but I'd like to see you get out of there.*

As if in answer, the door of the waiting room flew open and the fugitive charged out. But he was not alone. He was in the middle of a pack of seven or eight lads and one girl, who were clearly trying to protect him. The spectacle was almost comic: a gang of teenagers in black streetwear tearing along in the company of an old man—or rather, a sixteen-year-old dressed in a brown felt hat and brown overcoat.

"After them!" shouted Redvald. "Disable the bodyguards one by one, and then get Temple."

Chaos reigned on Platform 13. The parkour gang sprinted up the platform dodging travelers, vaulting luggage carts, and tic-tac-ing off station buildings. After them came the Knights of Akonio Dolo, running with less style but just as much speed. After them clumped two officers of the British transport police, who had arrived on the scene eager but bewildered.

"The train now at Platform 13 is the eighteen seventeen Southern Trains service to Brighton. Calling at East Croydon, Gatwick Airport, Three Bridges, Wivelsfield, Hassocks, Preston Park, and Brighton."

The Kinetix were good, but they were heavily outnumbered. Knights were flying at them from all directions, tripping and tackling, barging and grappling. One by one Temple's bodyguards were being taken down. Four of them had already bitten the concrete and only five remained.

Robin Redvald jogged along behind, feeling ever so smug. All that ghastly cloak-and-dagger stuff was over, and now he could hang back and enjoy the sight of Danny Temple being run to ground by eighty-five determined loonies. The boy had been offered a chance and refused to take it. *Be it on his own head.*

Commuters were piling onto the Brighton train, but Temple and his bodyguards did not attempt to board. Instead they konged a safety rail and skittered down the steps with the knights in hot pursuit. As Redvald followed, he noticed an orange cap next to the hat. *So Dupont is running with the pack, is he? So much the better.*

Six down, three to go. The only runners left were Temple, Dupont, and the long-haired blonde, running shoulder to shoulder along the brightly lit passageway. The sea of commuters parted before them, emitting cries of surprise and displeasure in a dozen languages.

Eager knights from other platforms were clattering down into the passage to join the hunt. Some turned up in front of the runners, making them dodge and duck as if their lives depended on it. *Why on earth did Temple come down here?* thought Robin Redvald. *He played right into our hands.*

A transport police officer appeared in front of the three fugitives, blocking their way. "Stop, I tell you!"

Dupont and the girl skidded to a halt but Temple ran on. He tic-tac-ed off the wall of the passageway and *jumped right over the policeman.* Not a leapfrog but a clear jump. Robin Redvald and the other knights watched open-mouthed as Temple landed behind the policeman and rolled on the concrete.

The few seconds that followed were ones that Robin Redvald was destined to replay in his mind over and over again. As Temple rolled, the brown hat fell off to reveal a shiny, shaven head.

"No!" cried the historian. *"It's not him!"*

The man in the brown overcoat looked about twenty years old and had an eyebrow piercing. Definitely not Danny Temple. And the lad in the orange cap was not Omar Dupont. He was about the right height but couldn't have been more than thirteen.

Redvald put a hand against the wall of the passageway to steady himself. *They changed clothes in the waiting room. They fooled us all.*

The officer of the transport police was turning purple. "You lot are a public nuisance," he fumed. "It's bad enough that you cause terror in the projects, but running wild in a public transport terminal is simply—simply—there's no excuse for it. And *you*"—turning to the man who wasn't Temple—"how *dare* you jump over me!"

"Sorry, officer," chirped the skinhead, picking up his hat. "I wasn't sure I could stop in time."

The officer's cheeks quivered in indignation. "You shouldn't have been running in the first place, should you? This passageway was here before you were born. What gives you the right to zoom along it like Stevenson's Rocket?"

The young man shrugged and his face broke into a grin. "They told me it was rush hour," he said.

The PA system bonged. "The train now departing from Platform 13 is the eighteen seventeen Southern Trains service to Brighton. Calling at East Croydon, Gatwick Airport . . ."

Gatwick Airport! Robin Redvald took off his baseball cap, threw it on the ground, and stamped on it. *Gatwick flipping Airport! They're going to try to leave the country. They're going after the gold!*

NINETEEN

Standing by the luggage racks, Danny pressed his nose to the window and watched Platform 13 slide out of sight. The adrenaline drained away and left him feeling miserable and empty.

"I told you the switch would work," said Omar.

"We got lucky."

"Luck had nothing to do with it," said Omar. "Misdirection, that's the key, like with all the best magic tricks. If you wave the hat around enough, no one notices the rabbit."

"All right then, Mr. Wizard," said Danny. "Why don't you do something really useful and magic us some plane tickets?"

"What?"

"Air France's night flight from London to Bamako costs over five hundred quid a seat. We don't have that kind of money."

"What about your freelance earnings?"

"I've got it all with me in cash. A hundred and fifty quid."

Omar curled his lip. "Is that all?"

Danny nodded and looked away. He was too proud to moan to Omar about his financial difficulties, but the truth was inescapable: However good a programmer he might be, his IT business was going nowhere fast.

"What about you?" asked Danny. "Got any savings stashed away?"

"No," said Omar. "And if I'd known you didn't either, I wouldn't have agreed to this Africa thing."

The silence that followed was long and awkward. Both boys gazed out the window at the city lights rushing past in a blur.

"There is one possibility," said Danny at last. "I could hack the Air France website and reserve a couple of tickets in our names."

Omar frowned. "That's a black-hat hack," he said. "I thought you didn't do black-hat."

"First time for everything," said Danny. "Problem is, my laptop's back at the flat."

"That's that, then," said Omar.

Danny turned and looked through the glass sliding door into the next car. "Have you ever noticed," he said slowly, "what a lot of train passengers carry laptops?"

Omar stared at him, horrified. "Oh, so you want to boost a laptop now, do you? We're not criminals, Danny!"

"We'll give it back when we're done with it," said Danny. "Come on, Grimps! Look into that car there. How many laptops do you see?"

"I'm not looking," said Omar.

"There's a kid just down there with a brand-new one," said Danny. "He's about fourteen years old, he's watching manga, and he's eating the biggest bag of crisps you've ever seen."

"I'm not listening."

"He's dropping crisp crumbs all over the keyboard. You've got to ask yourself, Grimps, does a kid like *that* deserve a computer like *that?*"

"La de daa," sang Omar with his fingers in his ears.

"Think of it as liberation. Mr. Toshi Ba is longing to be freed from a tedious life of manga and pickled onion crisps. He's longing to be put to nobler use, something worthy of his gigantic Centrino processor. I'm telling you, Grimps, hacking the Air France reservations system would bless that computer's heart."

Danny made his way into the next car and sat down opposite the crisp-eating boy. "Hello," he said. "My name's Kevin. Where are you going?"

"Brighton," said the boy, not looking up.

"Me, too," said Danny. "Give us a crisp."

The boy turned up the volume on his headphones and pretended not to have heard.

"I love manga!" shouted Danny.

"Good for you," said the boy. "Leave me alone."

Danny looked out the window at the trees flying past. A moment later Omar arrived, clutching handfuls of Coke cans and crisps from the café car. "Hey, Kevin," he said. "You'll never believe what just happened."

"What?" said Danny.

"They gave me all this stuff free."

"No!"

"I went to the café car for a can of Coke and the bloke behind the counter was, like, 'Help yourself, mate. Take whatever you want.'"

"How come?"

"They're bringing on new stock at Gatwick," said Omar. "He told me they have to get rid of all their current stock before the new stock comes on, what with EU regulations and all."

Danny glanced sideways and noticed the boy opposite him turning down the volume on his headphones. *Gotcha*.

"Cool!" Danny cracked open a can of Coke. "Here's to Europe!"

"Cheers!"

A passenger announcement came over the speaker. "This train will shortly be arriving at Gatwick Airport. Passengers leaving the train at this station are advised to take all their belongings with them. Gatwick Airport will be our next station stop."

The boy opposite Danny whipped off his headphones and fixed Omar with an accusing glare. "Is there anything left," he asked, "or did you take it all?"

"I took it all," said Omar, "except for the pickled onion crisps, of course. I wouldn't take those if you paid me."

"What?"

"No kidding. There's about fifty bags of pickled onion crisps that they can't shift. If no one claims them before the next stop, they're going to have to incinerate them."

"I'll claim them!" cried the boy.

"I wouldn't if I were you," said Omar. "Pickled onion crisps are a crime against humanity. Incineration's too good for them."

"Watch my stuff, just for a minute," said the boy, putting his manga on PAUSE. "I need to check on something."

As soon as the boy was out of sight, Danny put the laptop into its case and slung it over his shoulder; then he and Omar headed up the aisle away from the café car. As he walked, Danny unzipped the side compartment of the laptop and peered inside: It contained a PC card, a short Ethernet cable, and two manga DVDs.

"You've changed, Danny," said Omar, glancing nervously behind him. "A week ago, you'd never have done a thing like that."

"Funny old world," said Danny. "A week ago you'd never have helped me."

By the time the train pulled into the station, the boys were far away in the next-to-last car.

"This is Gatwick Airport. Please mind the gap."

Gatwick Airport. Last time Danny had been here was six months ago with Dad and the Melissa virus. Danny had come to see them off to their new life in Australia, and Dad had kept trying to persuade him to come with them. It had been an emotional day, and he didn't like even thinking about it.

Danny and Omar hurried off the train and straight onto the escalator marked DEPARTURES.

"Do you think onion boy will come after us?" asked Omar, glancing back over his shoulder.

"So what if he does?" said Danny. "What's he going to do, breathe on us?"

The departures hall on the second floor was massive but well signposted, and the boys soon found their way to the Air France information desk, where a pretty agent was dealing with an angry customer.

"I demand a refund," the customer was saying.

"I'm afraid that is impractical," said the agent. "The most I can do is—"

"Impractical!" shouted the customer. "What kind of a word is that? Do you mean illegal or do you mean inconvenient?"

"I fully appreciate the distress caused by the tarantula incident, sir. Please accept my sincere apologies, along with five hundred air miles for use on any Air France flight."

Danny let his eyes wander. There was a bundle of cables coming out of the back of the information desk and running all the way up the wall and along the ceiling beams. The thick red cable had to be the cat 5, or network cable. *If I could wire my laptop straight into that cat 5,* thought Danny, *I wouldn't need to worry about firewalls. I'd be behind them already!*

Danny backed away from the desk. "Tell me something, Grimps," he whispered. "Have you ever flown Air France?"

"Are you kidding?" said Omar. "I fly Air France every time I go to see my parents."

"Have you saved up any air miles?"

"No, I spend them as I go."

"But you do have an air mile account?"

"Sure."

"That's our way in," whispered Danny. "I'm guessing that the computer system controlling air miles is less secure than the reservations system. If I can splice onion boy's laptop onto the Air France intranet, I can put twenty thousand air miles straight into your account."

"What do you mean, *splice?*"

"I mean cut open the cat five cable and wire in the laptop. It's called a 'man in the middle' hack attack. I transfer the air miles and then you waltz up to the desk and buy our flights."

"I see." Omar looked completely baffled. "And Miss Air France over there isn't going to mind you splicing her cat five? Sounds painful to me."

"She's not going to see me," said Danny. "I'll be up there." He pointed at a round metal beam high up in the airport ceiling.

Omar puffed out his cheeks. "You want to balance that?"

"I've done higher in training."

"That was over water, Danny. Anyway, how would you get up there?"

Open your mind to parkour vision. Danny looked up and around and took a deep breath. "See the food court on the top level there?"

"Yes."

"Golden arches of McDonald's?"

"Yes."

"See how close they are to that diagonal ceiling beam?"

Omar chuckled and slapped his friend on the shoulder. "You're a legend, Danny. You go work your magic and I'll create a distraction. I'll be needing that jacket Baz gave you."

As the boys rode the escalator to Level 3, Danny shrugged off the yellow jacket and gave it to Omar. At the top they shook hands and parted ways. Danny strolled toward the golden arches, strapping the laptop bag tightly to his back. Omar flexed his fingers and prepared to put on a show.

Seated at one of the tables in the food court was a middle-aged woman with a little girl. The little girl had freckles and a ponytail, and she was halfway through a greasy burger the size of her head when something caught her attention.

"Look, Mummy! There's a man doing a handstand on the railing."

Omar was always doing handstands, but this one was special even for him. The rail he was balancing on separated the food court from a fifty-foot drop all the way down to the first-floor arrivals hall. Omar held himself there completely still and waited for an audience.

He did not have long to wait. People all over the food court were noticing the stunt and rising to their feet. Some reached for their cameras. Waiters and waitresses gasped and stared. Children giggled and pointed. And with everyone's attention on Omar, Danny climbed the golden arches.

TWENTY

The first few meters were hard work. Six consecutive muscle-ups made his injured wrist plead for mercy. But the climb got easier as the curve shallowed out, and in less than a minute Danny was at the zenith of the far arch.

Down below, Omar was showing off and loving every moment. He held the handstand for about half a minute and then ever so slowly lowered his feet until they touched down on the railing. He stood up straight, staring across the void with a gaze as cool as ice. "Three, two, one," he mouthed, then swung his arms and performed a spectacular back flip. The audience clapped and cheered as Omar landed neatly on the floor of the food court. They could not help themselves.

Unobserved upon his perch, Danny chuckled to himself. He had never bothered with free-run flips and tricks, having opted for a purer parkour philosophy: Get straight from A to B and overcome any obstacles en route. Crowd pleasers in parkour were like colored fonts in a computer program, as pointless as they were pretty. But right now he was glad of his friend's acrobatic eye candy. As Omar continued to cartwheel and somersault across the food court, Danny focused his full attention on the metal beam above his head. He bent his knees and jumped.

Ouch. The left wrist screamed again in protest at the muscle-up. *That's the last one,* he told himself. *From here on in it's all catting and hacking.*

Cat balance had been one of the first techniques Danny learned. He remembered practicing it along the footpath railings in Battersea Park before graduating to the parapet of the bridge. *Left palm, ball of right foot. Right palm, ball of left foot. Head down, back straight.* How many miles of cat balance had he accumulated over the last two years? Five? Fifty? Not to stop when you got it right, that was the thing. You had to practice until you couldn't get it wrong.

"Cat balance to the cat five," murmured Danny, crawling hand over hand toward the precious cables. This metal ceiling beam demanded exactly the same technique as the Battersea Park railings, except that up here the stakes were higher. A fall would be ten times farther, the ground would be harder, the screams of the public would be— *Don't even think about it. Concentrate on your technique. Cat to the cat and don't go splat.*

At last Danny reached the point where the balance beam crossed the airport wiring. He straddled the intersection, slid onion boy's computer out of its bag, and balanced it on his lap. A sudden murmur of conscience: *This is a black-hat hack. I don't do black-hat.*

Danny shrugged. *First time for everything.* He reached into his pocket and took out his penknife.

SwissFlash tools were well liked by hackers. A USB memory key nestled alongside the blade, and Danny's contained four gigabytes of data and hacking software. Danny inserted the key, booted into Linux, and installed his software.

"Scalpel," he murmured, unplugging the flash drive from the USB port and flipping out a small sharp blade. "Nurse, I'm going in." He cut four inches of casing from the cat 5 cable and deftly stripped the sheaths within to reveal eight copper wires. Then he did the same to the short Ethernet cable.

To connect the laptop to the network, each tiny cat 5 wire had to be twisted together with its Ethernet counterpart. *Orange to orange, pink to pink, white to white, fawn to fawn.* Danny linked the copper wires with nimble fingers. *Red to red, green to green, black to black, indigo to indigo. Bingo.*

He glanced down at the information desk. The crabby customer seemed to have cooled off and Miss Air France was busy on her computer, probably dealing with his compensation. Little did she suspect that she was about to be the object of a devastating man in the middle hack attack.

With one flick of his blade, Danny cut through the cat 5 cable between the two Ethernet entry points, and the stream of cat 5 information carriers rushed like lemmings along the diversion Danny had created for them—a diversion that ran right through his laptop. Danny felt a surge of triumph. *My name is*

Pergamon 256, king of hackers: Look on my works, ye Mighty, and despair!

Ethersniffer kicked in, and the screen filled with reams of information straight from Miss Air France's hijacked computer terminal. Danny was used to reading information dumps like this, so he quickly spotted the agent's username, CHANTAL_ MORET_, and her password, 0rland0.

"*Bonsoir,* Chantal," whispered Danny, glancing down at her. "Welcome to the Big Brother house."

He ran Wireshark to spoof the IP address of Chantal's terminal, accessed the intranet login page, and entered her username and password.

Welcome, Chantal!

If you are not Chantal Moret, please click **here.**

Danny punched the air. The "Flying Blue" Air Miles control panel awaited his instructions, and from this point the hack was as easy as falling off a log, or indeed a balance beam. It took just three minutes to find Omar Dupont in the database and to credit his account with twenty thousand air miles. "Be sure to extend every courtesy to this important client," Danny typed in the Comments section.

His mobile phone vibrated suddenly. The text message was from Omar, four words that made Danny's blood run cold: R & B HERE. Either Omar had developed a sudden interest in rhythm and blues or he had spotted Redvald and Bartholt somewhere in the airport.

GET TICKETS & MEET ME @ DEPTRS, Danny texted, then began to pack his tools into the laptop bag. The computer itself would have to stay where it was, of course. Unsplicing it now would break the connection, and they would never get those tickets.

Before he abandoned the computer, Danny found the owner's email address and memorized it. "I'll be in touch, onion boy," he whispered, balancing the laptop precariously on the metal beam. "Someday soon I'll pay you back in gold."

He edged back along the ceiling beam, dropped onto the golden arches, and began to slither down.

"Look, Mummy! That man's climbing down the big M."

The little girl's voice was shrill enough to attract everyone's attention. By the time Danny hit the floor of the food court, all eyes were on him.

"Don't mind me!" said Danny, waving. "Go on with your meals."

"Who the McFlurry are you?" shouted a stocky bus boy.

"I'm with the AED," said Danny. "Airport Environmental Department."

"But why—?"

"Pigeon in the ceiling beams. Nothing to worry about."

The bus boy put down his tray and frowned. "Where is it now?"

"Where is what?"

"The pigeon."

"Freed itself," said Danny. "Flew toward check-in. At least it won't be pooing on any Big Macs."

The bus boy muttered something inaudible, picked up his tray, and went back to work.

Danny stepped into an open lift and pressed the button marked LEVEL 2. As soon as the lift doors closed, he crumpled to the floor and put his head in his hands. The stress was getting the better of him.

I'm a con artist, a thief, and a black-hat, thought Danny. *I'm the lowest of the low. I'm no better than a virus writer.* He wished he had never gone to that HOPE convention. He wished he had never recovered that manuscript. He wished he had never heard of Akonio Dolo.

"Level Two: Departures," said a robotic female voice. The doors slid open, and there in front of him was Omar "Grimps" Dupont.

"Get up and follow me," said Omar. "There's plenty of time later for you to fall apart, but right now we have a plane to catch."

Danny didn't argue. He went with Omar, and together they scurried toward the departure gate like baby turtles toward the sea.

"If we can just get through this gate, we're home and dry," said Omar. "Redvald and Bartholt won't be able to get through without a ticket."

"You actually saw them?"

"Yes," said Omar. "The bad news is they're just over there by the newsstand."

Danny looked. Sure enough, Bartholt and Redvald were lurking behind the stand and spying on the departure gate.

"The good news," continued Omar, "is that they seem to be watching only the *end* of the line. We're going to cut in right at the front."

"How?"

"Just follow me and do what I do."

The official at the departure gate shook his head when he saw Omar and Danny trying to jump the line. "The end's back there," he said.

Omar gave a taut smile. "I know," he said, "but I can't hang around any longer. I've just signed autographs for half the people in this airport, and they've made me really late."

"Autographs?" The official scrutinized Omar's face. "Who are you?"

Omar handed over his passport and lowered his voice to a whisper. "Please don't say my name out loud—I've been mobbed quite enough already today."

"Your name means nothing to me—"

"Our tickets," said Omar, handing them to the official. Peering over Omar's shoulder, Danny noticed the words printed along the bottom. *Be sure to extend every courtesy to this important client.* Brilliant! He had never imagined that his little joke would end up printed on the actual ticket!

"I don't know if I should," said the official. "This is all very irregular."

Glancing at the end of the departure line, Danny saw Bartholt and Redvald pushing their way through the crowd toward them.

"How tiresome," said Omar, pointing at their pursuers. "More autograph hunters."

The official pursed his lips. "All right," he said. "Go on through, both of you."

Danny and Omar slipped through the departure gate and waited in line for the security check.

"Stop those boys!" Bartholt was shouting. "We want to talk to them."

"Well, you can't," snapped the official. "They're fed up with being hassled by the likes of you."

How right he is, thought Danny. He took off his shoes, placed them in the X-ray tray with the laptop bag, and stepped through the metal detector. He was feeling better already. By sheer skill and cunning he and Omar had escaped the knights, and now the adventure of a lifetime lay ahead of them—a journey to Africa and a quest for long-lost treasure.

"STOP!" The man at the X-ray machine stood up and pointed at Danny. "Hold it right there!"

"What's wrong?" stuttered Danny.

"Is this your bag?"

"Yes."

The man held up Danny's Swiss Army knife. "Did you really think you could board the plane with this?"

"I didn't th—"

"What do you think the bins back there are for?"

"For sharp ob—"

"I'm confiscating it, do you understand? And next time, be more careful when you pack your hand luggage."

"Of course. Thank you."

Danny and Omar took their bags and hurried on into the departure lounge. They both walked with a new spring in their step. The loss of Danny's treasured hacking tool was nothing compared to the excitement of finally being on their way.

Hacking and parkour are about one thing only: freedom. And strolling around the Gatwick departure lounge with only their phones and a bit of cash, the two boys felt freer than ever before.

TWENTY-ONE

Slowly up the moonlit river moved the pinasse. Seydou Zan, the boatman, was fast asleep with his head pillowed on a sugar sack, but Moktar Hasim was awake. He would not allow himself to sleep—not yet. He squatted on the hard deck, gazing at the stars and repeating over and over in his mind the proverb of King Suleymana: *A little sleep, a little slumber, a little folding of the hands to rest, and poverty will come upon you like a robber, penury like an armed warrior.*

From the village of Niafunké on the north bank of the river, the sound of a stringed instrument rose on the night air. A *kora*! Goosebumps rose on Moktar's skin. There was no sound on earth like the elegant flow of the *kora*'s twenty-one strings. Hypnotic filaments of harmony embroidered the night air and filled the fugitive's eyes with tears.

On the bow of the craft the river boy stood, lifting the wooden steering pole in and out of the water. Moktar Hasim looked at the boy and remembered himself as he once had been. Growing up in Bamako, Moktar had loved nothing more than to punt in the shallows of the Great River and to grope for catfish in the reeds. Now he got up and walked across the deck to where the river boy stood.

"You must be tired," he said gently. "Let me take the pole awhile."

The boy handed it to him. "It's heavy," he warned.

"Good," replied Moktar. "It is fitting for a man to have his strength tested."

Moktar Hasim lifted the pole, swung it with all his might, and whacked the river boy across the back of his knees, knocking him into the water with a loud splash. The boy gave a yelp of terror and starting swimming for the bank.

Seydou Zan opened his eyes where he lay, still half asleep.

"A little sleep," whispered Moktar, "a little slumber, a little folding of the hands to rest . . ."

He stepped toward Zan and swung the pole again, but the boatman's reflexes were better than his boy's. He rolled aside just in time, and his sugar-sack pillow exploded under the impact of Moktar's pole. The next blow glanced off the boatman's thigh and splintered the planks on the bow of the pinasse.

The boatman's eyes blazed in the moonlight. He limped to the far side of the vessel, grabbed a fish knife and a net, and turned to face his enemy, sinews stiffening, ready to pounce.

Moktar smirked. "Good weapons, gladiator," he said, "but you'll be dead in the water before you have a chance to use them." He took three short steps forward, adjusted his grip on the steering pole, and hurled it javelin style with all his might. The pole passed straight through the weave of the net and struck the boatman in the chest. He hit the deck of the pinasse hard and did not get up.

"Not much of a fight," said Moktar, moving forward and standing over him. "Very one-sided, just like our card games used to be."

"My chest," gasped Seydou Zan. "I can't breathe."

"Shocking," said the fugitive, "but not surprising. I would guess that you have two or three broken ribs and perhaps a punctured lung." He dropped to one knee and felt Zan's pulse.

"Why have you done this to me?" croaked the boatman.

"Because of the manuscript," said Moktar.

"What manuscript?"

"The one you were planning to take from me."

"I don't know what you're talking about."

"Yes, you do."

Moktar unbuttoned the boatman's shirt, eased it off him, and laid it to one side. Then he unstrapped the watch from the boatman's wrist and put it on his own. The time was seven minutes past midnight.

"I don't want to die," croaked Zan.

"Of course you don't," murmured Moktar. He took the boatman gently under the armpits and heaved him over the side of the pinasse into the river.

TWENTY-TWO

The Maison des Jeunes in Bamako was a three-story concrete monstrosity popular with Rastas, backpackers, and mosquitoes. Danny and Omar's room was two flights up overlooking the River Niger and the old Pont des Martyrs.

Not that they were interested in the Pont des Martyrs. They lay on their beds swatting at mosquitoes and glugging water out of two-liter plastic bottles. They felt as hot as baked potatoes and culture-shocked to the eyeballs. It was eleven o'clock in the morning.

"Five bites and counting," groaned Danny. "How many more bites do I need for these little fellas to give me malaria?"

"It's not the fellas that give you malaria," said Omar. "It's the girls you've got to worry about—female *Anopheles* mosquitoes. And not all of those carry the virus, either. It depends on lots of factors, so the best thing is to try and avoid getting bitten at all."

"Check you out," said Danny. "Chief Malaria Lecturer at the London School of Tropical Medicine, are you?"

"No," said Omar. "I'm just someone who didn't quit school at sixteen to do freelance IT."

Danny clapped at a mosquito and missed. "What is that supposed to mean?"

"It means that I could drive a tank through the gaps in your general knowledge. Do you ever wish you hadn't dropped out?"

"I didn't drop out. I went into business."

"Business!" Omar took a long swig of water. "Not exactly a dot-com millionaire, are you?"

"What?"

"Yesterday, when you said your total savings were a hundred and fifty pounds, I thought you were joking. What's a hundred and fifty quid good for? One night at an average London hotel."

"Shut up."

"Or a month in this Maison de Hell."

Danny sat up and swung his legs over the side of the bed. "What's gotten into you?" he said. "You been bitten by any mad dogs recently?"

"Must have been," said Omar, "or I wouldn't have agreed to come to this stupid place. I'm going to get into nightmare trouble when my parents find out, and you're going to blow your pathetic savings, and for what? The nothing chance of finding a pot of lost gold at the end of a rainbow. You're like some gummy-eyed gambler, desperate to make good his losses with a big win. You're pathetic."

Danny grabbed a ten-pence coin off his bedside table and

jumped to his feet. "Here's an idea," he said. "Heads, I go for a walk. Tails, I stay here and smash your face in."

"Make my day," said Omar.

Danny tossed the coin and caught it. "Heads," he said. "Lucky you—I'll see you later."

"Where are you going?"

"Shopping," said Danny. "Get some sleep, Mad Dog—it'll do you good."

Danny slammed the door on his way out. He went along the corridor, down two flights of steps, and out into the scorching sunlight. Six Malian lads were sitting on the low concrete wall outside the hostel. They wore colorful Rasta berets and were passing a smoldering cigarette from one to another. They jumped up when they saw Danny.

"*Salut, mon ami!*" said one of them, and began to prattle in rapid street French. He stopped when he saw Danny's blank expression.

"*Parlez-vous anglais?*" said Danny.

A wiry lad in a football shirt stepped forward and took off his beret. "I speak English small-small," he said. "Do you want drumming lesson?"

"No, thank you."

"Do you want camel ride?"

"No," said Danny. "I want to change some money. Is there a bank near here?"

The lad nodded quickly. "Yes, yes. I will take you to a very big bank."

Danny followed the boy down a little side street, past a shoe-repair stall and a kiosk selling coffee and bread. A roadside radio was blaring out reggae, and he couldn't help walking in time to the beat.

"What's your name?" asked Danny.

"Thierry," said the boy. "What's yours?"

"Danny."

"Where are you from, Danny?"

"England."

To Danny's surprise, Thierry immediately broke into song to the tune of "Que Sera Sera."

"Steve Gerrard Gerrard," sang Thierry, "can blast it from forty yards. He's big and he's diamond hard, Steve Gerrard Gerrard!"

"Who taught you that?" Danny asked, laughing.

"English tourists. They taught me others, too."

A young man in a blue coverall was crouching beside the road, holding an inner tube over a small flame. He looked up and waved as Danny and Thierry walked past.

"People here are very friendly," said Danny.

"All the tourists say that," said Thierry.

They came out onto another wide street. Severed goat heads grinned at them from a butcher's stall. Mopeds and taxis rattled along the streets. Thierry pointed up at a multistory eyesore topped by enormous concrete bat ears. A sign above the entrance read BANK OF AFRICA.

"Thanks for your help," said Danny.

"No problem," said Thierry. "I will wait here for you."

Changing money took longer than Danny had expected. He had to wait in line for half an hour, then wait another twenty minutes while his passport was photocopied. At last the cash arrived—a thick wad of purple notes, 124,000 West African francs.

When Danny emerged into the sunlight, he found Thierry sitting on the steps of the bank. He was flicking his lighter on and off, and singing "You'll Never Walk Alone."

"Good song for a tourist guide," said Danny.

Thierry shrugged. "Where next?" he asked.

"The main market."

The *grand marché* in Bamako was a bewildering labyrinth of shops and stalls, but Thierry knew it inside out. They wandered from one merchant to another, browsing and haggling, and before long Danny had bought everything he and Omar needed: a backpack, flip-flops, mosquito nets, sunglasses, flashlights, cotton slacks, SIM cards, and a *Mali on the Cheap* guidebook. He even managed to find four packets of his favorite sweet biscuits, custard creams. All together his purchases came to 22,000 francs—about 25 pounds.

"Where next?" said Thierry.

"Is there a cybercafé in town?"

"Sure." Thierry waved airily. "There's one just across the road there."

Danny handed him a thousand-franc note. "Thanks for your help. Don't bother waiting for me."

Cybermania was full of computers, teenagers, potted plants, and mirrors. Ceiling fans whirred lazily. Hard drives chuntered. Flies buzzed. A glassy-eyed *gérante* pointed her chin toward a free computer. *"Allez-y,"* she said yawning.

Danny sat down at the terminal and flexed his fingers. The keyboard was French, so a few letters were in unfamiliar places, but that was a small price to pay for being reconnected after all this time. He felt like a camel arriving at an oasis.

There were 650 new messages in Danny's inbox, and almost all of them were Facebook friend requests. Danny logged into his Facebook account and scrolled down the list of would-be friends, clicking "Ignore" on each one.

On an impulse he clicked onto the Knights of Akonio Dolo Facebook group, and what he saw there made his stomach churn. Membership of the group was now up to *3,000 people*, and the discussion forum was rife with gossip and speculation. Danny clicked on a recent post entitled GATWICK AIRPORT LAPTOP CLUE.

New post by **Mordecai Kemp** at **5:22 a.m.**

Get this, you lot—the following story broke on News 24 at 3 o'clock this morning: "Check-in halls at Gatwick were evacuated at midnight when a traveler alerted airport authorities about a suspicious object in the ceiling beams. Bomb disposal droid i-BOD was sent up to investigate and found the offending object to be a harmless laptop computer. The computer had allegedly been used to hack into the airport intranet and purchase two plane tickets to West Africa."

If you ask me, that sounds like the work of Danny Temple. He hasn't gone to stay with Dupont's parents at all. He's gone to MALI to look for the gold—which means he must have CRACKED THE SQUARE! If we have any hope of reaching an endgame with DT, we need to get knights to Mali FAST.

Reply posted by **Ed Potts** at **8:45 a.m.**

Re: Gatwick Airport laptop clue

Good work, Mordecai. My older brother is in West Africa right now as part of his gap year. He's cycling through Burkina Faso, Mali, Ivory Coast, Ghana, Togo, Benin, and Niger, and guess which country he is in now—MALI! I emailed him a bunch of KOAD stuff and told him to hunt down Danny Temple. I know he'll be up for it, 'cause he loves mystery and adventure even more than I do. Wouldn't want to be DT right now—hehe.

Reply posted by **Zwiebel Zwo** at **9:03 a.m.**

Re: Gatwick Airport laptop clue

Forgive my broken English. I am an anthropology student at the University of Tübingen but am presently making research in Bamako, capital of Mali. I heard about the Akonio Dolo legend since a long time and your quest interests me. If the runaway boys are here in Bamako, they will not be complicated to uncover—I shall pursue enquiries at some of the cheap hostels in town and reply back to you.

Danny did not read the rest of the thread. He jumped up from his chair, slapped five hundred francs on the counter, and ran out of the cybercafé. He had not expected the tentacles of KOAD to reach so far so fast. If they already had someone searching the city's cheap hostels, it could not be long before they started poking around the cheapest of the lot: the Maison des Jeunes. He had to warn Omar!

Danny sprinted back the way he had come—past the grinning goat heads, the mechanic, the coffee-and-bread kiosk, and the shoe-repair stall. Left along the riverbank he ran, then left again into the shabby portico of the Maison des Jeunes. The Rasta boys outside the hostel called out to him as he passed, and he mumbled a greeting in return.

Inside the hostel a white man in a suit was leaning on the front desk chatting to the receptionist. Danny had no idea what a German anthropologist should look like, but there was something about this visitor that made him uneasy. The white shirt collar and spotless linen suit seemed out of place in this scruffy joint. Could this be Zwiebel Zwo, the anthropologist-knight, pursuing his enquiries?

Danny ran up the stairs and along the corridor. "Time to go, Grimps," he said, bursting into the room.

Omar opened his eyes and frowned. "I was having such a nice dream," he murmured, "and you weren't in it at all."

"Listen," said Danny. "The knights are on to us."

Omar sat up and blinked hard. "They can't be. You said we'd be safe once we'd left London."

"Guess I was wrong. There are at least two knights already in Mali, and one of them is down in reception as we speak."

"I see." Omar started to put on his running shoes. "So it's goodbye, Maison des Jeunes?"

"Yes."

"Farewell, mosquitoes?"

"Yes."

"Gutted."

The boys threw their meager possessions into the backpack, ran out into the corridor, and headed for the roof.

TWENTY-THREE

The sun descended vermilion and orange over the River Niger. Moktar Hasim stood on the bow of his stolen pinasse, plunging the steering pole into the river's silty depths. The top of the pole was flecked with blood.

Having dumped the dying merchant overboard, Moktar had removed his burqa disguise and donned the shirt of his victim. Now he heartily regretted the change. With every single gust of wind the fabric seemed to clutch his skin in chilling reprimand. *Less dreadful,* thought Moktar, *to be humiliated in the clothes of a woman than to be tormented in the clothes of a dead man.*

He shivered and scowled at the horizon. For two nights and two days he had lived on this cursed river. The drinking water in the canister was warm and stale, and the only food left to him was a handful of peanuts and one cob of corn. These meager rations would have to last another twenty-four hours until he moored in old Mopti town.

My patience will be rewarded, thought Moktar. *When I arrive in Mopti tomorrow night, I will go straight to Chez Maman for a plate of grilled chicken and a jug of millet beer, and then I will go to the house of marabout Al Haji Bukari Musa.*

Ever since his childhood in Bamako, Moktar had heard the name of Al Haji Bukari Musa—the oldest and most fearsome leader in the whole length of the Niger, unrivaled in power and depth of insight. People came to Al Haji from all over Mali with all sorts of problems—lost camels, wicked stepmothers, bullying co-wives, dizzying toothaches—and they invariably went away with a spring in their step. If anyone alive could decipher the magic square, it was Al Haji Bukari Musa.

Moktar touched the scroll around his neck and raised his eyes to the heavens. *Hear my prayer, O Merciful and Compassionate One, and carry me to Mopti. Incline the will of the marabout to aid me in my quest. Scramble a fleet of brainy djinns to penetrate the square. Grant me, your servant, a sound mind, a pure heart, and a steadfast spirit, and LET ME GET THAT GOLD!*

TWENTY-FOUR

Five hundred kilometers upriver in Bamako, Danny and Omar were crouching underneath the Pont des Martyrs, watching the sunset. They had parkoured seven roofs, clambered down a mango tree, and crossed over the bridge in the back of a donkey cart, unnoticed even by the driver. They could still see the upper floors of the Maison des Jeunes across the river, but hidden here in the shadows, they knew they were safe. All in all, it had been an A-star escape.

"Parkour in flip-flops!" Danny chuckled. "That's skill for you."

"No, it's not," snapped Omar, whose mood showed no sign of improvement. "Parkour is not for prats, Danny. Next time, you will follow my instructions and leave your flipping flip-flops behind."

"Run in bare feet, you mean?"

"If you have to, yes."

Danny picked up a small flat stone and skimmed it across the surface of the river. "It doesn't matter," he said. "We're both fine."

"Really? Are you talking metric fine or imperial fine? Not-dead-yet fine or not-got-anywhere-to-sleep-tonight fine?"

"We'll find somewhere," said Danny. "There are lots of cheap hostels in town."

"All of which are being eyeballed by Evil von Zweebil or whatever his name is."

"Well then, we go to an expensive hotel."

"And blow our entire budget in one night."

"Well then, we hang up our mosquito nets right here under this bridge."

"Good thinking, Temple." Omar rolled his eyes.

"Listen," said Danny. "I've had it up to here with your negativity, so if you're planning to continue this Despondent Dupont Glass-Half-Empty road show, then you can just—"

He was interrupted by a tinny ringtone coming from his backpack. It was the phone he had bought a SIM card for *that very morning*. How could that be? He had not given his new number to anyone.

"Don't answer it," warned Omar.

"Why not?" said Danny. "It's probably a wrong number."

"A trap more like," said Omar. "Have you never heard of mobile phone triangulation? You can track down anyone on earth by triangulating their mobile phone signals."

"Don't talk rubbish," said Danny, rummaging in his bag for his phone. When he answered it, he recognized the voice immediately. "Thierry!" he cried. "How on earth did you get this number?"

"*Salut,* Danny. I was right beside you when you bought your SIM card, remember?"

"Oh yes. So what's up?"

"I saw you and your friend on the roof of the Maison des Jeunes. I thought maybe you have trouble."

"It's a trap," hissed Omar, who was listening in on the conversation. "Hang up!"

"We do have trouble, Thierry," said Danny. "Accommodation trouble. We really need a place to sleep tonight."

"Come and stay with my family," said Thierry straightaway. "We like visitors."

"Barbecued or boiled?" muttered Omar in the background.

"Thank you, Thierry," said Danny. "We accept."

"Good, I'll come and get you. Where are you?"

"We're under the—"

"Don't tell him!" urged Omar.

"Under the Pont des Martyrs, across the river from the hostel."

"Stay there. My brother and I will pick you up."

Twenty minutes later Thierry and his brother arrived on two rickety P50 mopeds. They stopped just long enough for Danny and Omar to climb on; then off they sped again, wobbling precariously through the back streets of Bamako and belching evil black smoke in their wake. Not long after, they roared into a mud-brick compound and slammed on the brakes.

"Bamako Ritz," Thierry announced with a grin. "And here comes the owner."

A large round woman hurried out of the house and welcomed Danny and Omar like long-lost sons. She gave them each a bowl of warm goat's milk to drink and put a bucket of water around the back of the house for them to wash with.

The evening meal was a boiling-hot dumpling made from millet flour, herbs, and water. Danny and Omar ate with Thierry's father and brother, crouched round one enormous dish and taking turns to break off pieces of dumpling. The millet dough burned Danny's fingers and the roof of his mouth, but it tasted delicious. It felt funny to be eating dinner with a real family. It had been a long time.

Thierry laid two thin plastic mats on the ground under a spreading mango tree and helped Danny and Omar hang up their mosquito nets.

"Do you still think it's a trap?" whispered Danny to Omar as he tucked the netting under the corners of his mat.

"Definitely," murmured Omar. "But I'm too tired to care anymore. Good night, bro."

"Good night."

"What is a verb, children?" Miss Bassett was pacing the classroom, smelling of coconut.

"Speak up," she lisped. "Who's going to tell me what a verb is?"

"A verb is a doing word, miss."

"Very good. And who can give me an example of a verb?"

A porcupine of hands. "Miss, miss, please, miss, I can, miss!"

"Run, miss!"

"Jump, miss!"

"Climb, miss!"

"Excellent verbs, children. Well done!"

Danny opened his eyes and saw the canopy of his mosquito net and the bright green leaves of the mango tree above it. He had been dreaming. Or perhaps remembering.

A scraggy-necked vulture was sitting on a mango branch, examining Danny with its head on one side.

"What's up, baldy?" he said to the vulture. "Never seen a white boy before?"

The smell of dust in the air made Danny look around. Thierry's mother was already hard at work, sweeping the yard with a short-handled broom. A gang of guinea fowl followed her, jabbering furiously to one another. Above the screech of the guinea fowl and the scratch of the broom came the sound of raucous song:

> "I am a Liverpudlian
> I come from the Spion Kop
> I like to sing, I like to shout
> I get thrown out quite a lot."

"I bet you do!" shouted Danny. "*Bonjour*, Thierry!"

"*Bonjour*," said Thierry, strolling over. "*Tu as bien dormi?*"

"Not bad, thanks. Except for the wild dogs howling at two o'clock in the morning, the cockerels crowing at three o'clock, the donkeys braying at four o'clock, the call to prayer at five o'clock, and the Liverpool terrace chants at six o'clock."

"You overslept," said Thierry. "The Bandiagara bus leaves in fifteen minutes."

Danny dismantled his mosquito net and kicked Omar to wake him up. They shared a hurried breakfast of millet pancakes and coffee and thanked Thierry's mother for her kindness.

"God go with you," she said, raising her palms in supplication.

Thierry and his brother whisked Danny and Omar to the bus station on their P50s and arrived with only minutes to spare.

The Bandiagara bus was not a bus. It was a minibus. It was crammed full of people and piled high on top with mopeds, sacks of rice, traveling bags, calabashes, and chickens. A curly-horned ram was enthroned on top of it all, grinning into the wind like a deranged despot.

"Get on, get on," urged Thierry. "Find a place to sit, quickly."

Danny pushed his way onto the bus and sat down in the aisle on top of a large canister of what smelled like gasoline. Omar got on after him, shaking his head as if to wake himself from a bad dream. Thierry's face appeared at the window to Danny's right. "You'll be in Bandiagara before you know it," he called. "Enjoy your sightseeing."

Danny took off his watch and handed it to Thierry, along with a packet of custard creams.

Thierry beamed. "Take this," he said, passing Danny his lighter. "Souvenir of Bamako."

Danny put the lighter in his pants pocket. The bus driver started the engine and hooted the horn to announce departure. The last few passengers piled onto the bus.

"Bon voyage!" shouted Thierry. "Hope in your heart!"

Danny touched his fist to his chest. "Never walk alone!" he replied.

The bus grated into first gear and they were off. As they slalomed through the narrow streets, the pile of baggage on the roof rack swayed precariously. Danny held on to the sides of his gas canister so tightly that his knuckles whitened. He found himself imagining a head-to-head rally race between Inspector Carp and this Bandiagara bus driver. It would be a close thing.

"How long is this journey going to take?" asked Omar, who was squished between a sack of millet and a very large African lady. The lady had a baby at her breast and a cockerel at her feet.

"Let me see," said Danny, flicking through his *Mali on the Cheap* guidebook. "Bamako to Mopti: twelve hours. Mopti to Bandiagara: four hours. Total: sixteen hours."

Omar wriggled in his seat and scowled. "Sixteen hours!" he cried. "*Sixteen hours* on a minibus with a toe-sucking rooster at my feet!"

"It's an adventure!" said Danny. "Who else at school gets to spend their half-term holiday hunting for hidden treasure?"

"Yes, you're loving it, aren't you?" said Omar. "You're never happier than when you're cooped up in a small space with dozens of sweaty bodies and nothing to do but think—it's just like being at a HOPE convention."

"Come on, Grimps," said Danny. "Aren't you even a little bit excited? Look around you, man—you're in Africa!"

"And wishing I was in France," said Omar. "Sorry to burst your bubble, mate, but this so-called holiday is the pits. I'd rather be hanging upside down off the Eiffel Tower, painting the girders with a toothbrush. At least that way I'd get some fresh air!"

TWENTY-FIVE

Fresh air was not in short supply for Moktar Hasim. While Danny and Omar were rattling along in their overloaded minibus, Moktar continued his solitary river journey under a measureless African sky, the manuscript around his neck as hot and heavy as a noose. It was late afternoon.

He had now spent three nights and three days on this pinasse, and he was hurting. Early this morning he had finished off the corn and peanuts and drained the last drop of drinking water, and since then he had been at the mercy of those demonic twins hunger and thirst. At midday, driven to distraction by his cracked lips and parched throat, he had gulped several mouthfuls of the filthy river water. It only made him vomit.

As the afternoon wore on, Moktar began to see other boats on the river. Fishermen waved affably to him and called out afternoon greetings and blessings, but to Moktar's tortured mind they appeared as rabid djinns and leering hobgoblins, floating alongside to taunt him with obscene gestures and prophecies of doom.

Eventually the pinasse arrived at a fork in the river.

"Take a right!" gibbered a djinn. "Love of money is the root of all evil! Abandon your quest!"

"Take a left!" howled a hobgoblin. "Go on down to Mopti! Embrace your destiny."

Moktar stabbed the steering pole deep into the silt and swung the pinasse left. He was going mad—he could feel it happening with every minute that passed.

The minarets of old Mopti town glided into view. Mopti, jewel of the Niger! Mopti, oasis of grilled chicken and millet beer! Mopti, abode of Al Haji Bukari Musa—the man to whom Akonio Dolo's manuscript would surely surrender its secrets.

TWENTY-SIX

We're not far from Mopti," said Danny. "The guidebook reckons it's one of the most picturesque towns in Mali. It's built on three islands and it's got a massive harbor—hundreds of colorful fishing canoes and merchant craft all tied up in rows. Except we won't see any of it because it'll be dark by the time we get there."

Omar raised his eyebrows but did not reply. He was gazing out the window at a herd of long-horned cows being chivvied along by a small boy.

"By the way," said Danny, "you were spot on yesterday when you called me a failure. One hundred percent correct. Congratulations."

Omar turned round. "I didn't call you a failure," he said.

"You said I wasn't exactly a dot-com millionaire, and you were right. I earn just enough to live on and sometimes not even that. If my father wasn't paying my rent, I'd be out on the street by now."

Omar shifted uneasily in his seat. "Don't exaggerate," he muttered.

"I gambled and I lost," continued Danny. "I thought I could land a cool job as a security consultant, like that kid who hacked NASA. But it just hasn't happened for me. And now I want to make good my losses with one big win, just like you said."

"Don't worry about it," said Omar. "You'll be fine."

"Metric fine or imperial fine?"

"Both." Omar grinned. "You cracked the square, didn't you?"

"So what if I did? Who's to say that the gold is still where Akonio Dolo hid it? Who's to say it was ever there in the first place? What if Dolo was just having a laugh at his enemies' expense?"

"It'll be there," said Omar.

Danny shook his head. "You know what, Grimps? Ever since Bartholt chucked that chimney pot through my skylight, I've been running so hard I've hardly had time to think. This bus was just what I needed to bring me back to earth. You were right, mate—we're on a wild goose chase. I'm sorry I got you involved."

"I'm not sorry," said Omar. "I'm spending my half-term holiday treasure hunting in Africa—that's off-the-scale cool. And like I say, I reckon the gold is still there."

"After seven hundred years?" Danny shook his head. "It will be a miracle if we find anything. It'll be like trawling the Welsh lakes for King Arthur's sword."

"Stop talking like a wuss," said Omar. "Have a custard cream—it'll do you good."

TWENTY-SEVEN

Moktar sat back in his seat and smiled. The chicken at Chez Maman had been grilled to perfection and the millet beer was wonderfully restorative. He paid for his meal and asked the serving girl for directions to the house of Al Haji Bukari Musa.

The girl shuddered when she heard the marabout's name. "It's in the old town," she said, "in the shadow of the Grand Mosque."

"Thank you," said Moktar Hasim. He glided out into the cool of the evening and crossed the dike that led to the old part of town. The streets here were narrow and labyrinthine, but the towering minaret was a prominent landmark, and it did not take Moktar long to locate the marabout's house.

"Kok-kok!" called Moktar Hasim, clapping his hands in the courtyard. "Are you passing the evening in peace, Al Haji?"

The wooden front door creaked open and Al Haji Bukari Musa stood before him on the threshold. "Peace only," said the old man, fixing Moktar with a keen gaze as they shook hands. "How are your colleagues in Timbuktu?"

Moktar blinked and took a step backward. *What did you say?*

"You work in Timbuktu, do you not?"

"I might."

"And you have been steering someone else's pinasse. That makes you either very kind or—" The marabout stopped short. "In the name of God, what have you done? Have you killed a man?"

"No more soothsaying!" cried Moktar. "Have I not been alone with my guilt these last two days and nights? I did not come here to be told my past."

"Then why did you come?"

"I need counsel."

"Do you intend to harm me?"

"Of course not."

"Then you are wise," said the old man. "Come in." He ushered Moktar into his hut and pointed to a wicker chair. "Sit."

Moktar sat. *So the rumors are true,* he thought. *When Al Haji Bukari Musa looks at you, he reads the secrets of your soul.*

The marabout shut the door, plunging the room into darkness. "You're a bad man, Monsieur Hasim," he said.

Moktar almost fell off his chair. "You know my name!"

"Of course."

"Then you also know about—?"

"The manuscript mugging? Yes, I know about that."

"I fear you, old man."

A match flared in the darkness and the old man lit a kerosene lamp. Apart from the lamp, the chair, and one shelf of tattered books, the room was completely bare. *And there was not a single window.*

"All of Mopti is talking about the manuscript mugging," said the marabout. "Show me this famous manuscript that is worth a man's life."

Moktar put his hand to the string around his neck. He knew the marabout was his best chance of solving the square, but at the same time he had a strong desire to keep it to himself. Reluctantly, he drew the scroll up over his head, untied it, and gave it to the old man.

The marabout took the parchment in trembling hands. "If I help you," he said, "what will be my reward?"

"A quarter of Akonio Dolo's gold shall be yours," said Moktar.

The marabout nodded his assent and crouched down next to the flickering light of the kerosene lamp. *"Bismillahi,"* he whispered, narrowing his eyes to study the manuscript. "Ah yes, what have we here? Hail to the Nommo, heavenly ancestor. Monitor, Teacher, Master of the Water!"

Moktar Hasim started. "You recognize the Nommo?"

"I have big ears," said the old man, not looking up from the paper. "Everyone from here to Niafunké is talking about Dogons and Dolos and ancestral Nommos. I told you the manuscript mugging was big news."

Moktar felt a bead of cold sweat run down his forehead. He wanted to leap up out of the chair and run away. Out of this house, out of this town, preferably out of this world.

"Quickly," he said. "What can you tell me about the square?"

"Seven by seven," said the old man, "with the names of the four archangels inscribed along the sides. This is the square of the planet Zuhra."

"What does that mean?"

"It means eggs," said the marabout. "Do you like eggs, Moktar Hasim?"

"I don't mind them."

The marabout looked up and began to chant. With his face lit from beneath by the orange lamp, the hollow eye sockets and cheekbones gave his face a decidedly eerie aspect.

> "Scratch Zuhra on a silver plate
> Behind the hen coop facing west
> Then watch my chickens levitate
> And shower eggs into the nest."

Moktar felt suddenly and unaccountably terrified. He jumped to his feet and yelled at the marabout. "Don't waste my time with talk of levitating chickens! Your chickens can levitate to the treetops for all I care! I want gold!"

"Sit down," said the old man, and there was steel in his voice.

Moktar Hasim sat down.

"I was about to say," said Al Haji Bukari, "that you could scratch this square on a hundred plates of purest Zindar silver and not one of your chickens would levitate an inch. And you know why not?"

"Because I don't *believe*," sneered Moktar.

"Yes," said the old man gravely. "And also because the square is wrong."

"Wrong? How can it be wrong? That square is from a fourteenth-century al-Kabari textbook."

"Which is precisely why it's wrong. I must say, I'm disappointed in you, Moktar Hasim. If you knew anything about fourteenth-century Timbuktu, you would know that al-Kabari included a deliberate error in each of his magic squares."

"Why?"

"Two very good reasons. Firstly, the inclusion of an error taught students to analyze their squares carefully and not to take anything for granted. A good scholar never takes anything for granted, as you of all people should know. Secondly, and more importantly, it guarded against"—the marabout lowered his voice to a whisper—"*accidental magical occurrences.* True magic squares are powerful beasts, and when you mess with them, you can end up getting hurt."

"Is that so?"

"Of course. Take the case of Faskia al-Faskia and the Bandiagara bees, for example. Little Faskia was sitting in the branches of a baobab tree messing about with some magic squares, when he accidentally dropped the square of the planet Merrikh down into the hollow of the tree. A moment later, a swarm of magic bees came out of the hollow and—"

"I don't have time for this," hissed Moktar Hasim. "Just tell me what the square means!"

The marabout stood up and handed back the scroll. "Your lack of patience is precisely the reason you have not already discovered this manuscript's secret. You call yourself a scholar, Moktar Hasim, but all I see before me is a little boy throwing tantrums. Be quiet and let me tell you what Mohammed ibn Mohammed al-Fulani al-Kishnawi used to say to his students: 'When working with magic squares, do not give up, for that is ignorance and not according to the rules of this art. You cannot hope to achieve success without infinite perseverance.'" The marabout put a hand on Moktar's shoulder. "Come, my son, do not give up. Let your blood run cool, and look at the square again."

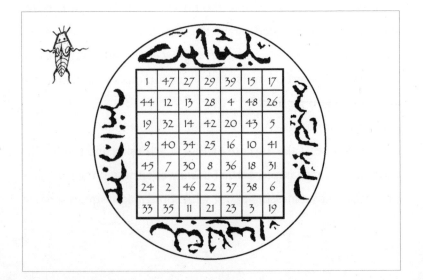

Moktar Hasim stared sulkily at the grid, letting his eyes run up and down the columns and along the rows. The words of the Fulani master echoed in his mind: *You cannot hope to achieve success without infinite perseverance.*

After what seemed like a very long time indeed, he noticed something. "That's odd," he said. "There are two nineteens."

The marabout clapped his hands and did a little skip. "Why is that odd, Moktar Hasim?"

"Because all the other numbers in the square appear only once."

The marabout whooped and pirouetted. "Dig down!" he cried. "Quarry deep, and a spring of knowledge will gush forth."

Moktar bent his head to examine the rows and columns that contained the nineteens. "It doesn't add up," he murmured. "The numbers in the very last row don't add up to one hundred seventy-five. They add up to one hundred forty-five."

"And the columns?" prompted the marabout, hopping from foot to foot. "Dig down, Moktar Hasim. Knowledge is power!"

Moktar frowned down at the manuscript. "The last column is short as well. The last row and the last column are both thirty short."

The old man clapped his hand to his mouth in feigned amazement. "Are you telling me we have an impostor in our square?"

"Yes," said Moktar, beginning to gain in confidence. "The impostor is this nineteen down here in the bottom right corner. For the square to work, the nineteen should be forty-nine!"

"Allahu Akbar!" The marabout raised his hands in praise, then suddenly bent down so that his mouth was next to Moktar's ear. "Now that your blood is running cool, prepare to ask yourself the two-million-mithqal question: Where did Akonio Dolo hide his gold?"

Moktar Hasim panicked. He was so close to the big break-through that his mind fogged up completely. *Dig down, Hasim,* he told himself. *Knowledge is power.* But only when he opened his mouth to speak did his mind begin to clear. "Legend has it," he said slowly, "that before Akonio Dolo died, he scaled the Sankore mosque and confessed his theft to the world. He declared that the gold was hidden in a secret chamber in the Bandiagara cliffs, nineteen ghalva northeast of Tireli. And then he talked of a key."

"What is the key, scholar?"

"The key is the square marked with the sign of the Nommo. In this square, nineteen is not nineteen. *Nineteen is forty-nine.*"

"Therefore?"

"Therefore Akonio Dolo hid his gold in a secret chamber *forty-nine ghalva northeast of Tireli.*"

"And how long is a ghalva, scholar?"

"One ghalva is seven hundred twenty Arabic feet," said Moktar. "About two hundred thirty meters."

The marabout went to the corner of the room and picked up a calabash of millet water. "Let us drink a toast," he said. "You are about to become the richest man in Mali."

"And you the second richest," said Moktar, taking the calabash and smiling for the first time in five days. "To Akonio Dolo!"

"Akonio Dolo!"

The two men drank together like old friends, and when the calabash was empty, Moktar stood up to leave.

"Before I go," he said, "there is something I must know."

"Ask," said the marabout.

"Who told you all those things about me? Was it the djinns of the air or the djinns of the water?"

"Neither," said the marabout. "Your right hand told me."

Moktar stared. "What do you mean?"

The old man hesitated. "I do not usually reveal my methods," he said.

"Go on," urged Moktar. "You can trust me."

"Very well, then." The marabout gave a mischievous grin. "When we shook hands on the threshold, I felt blisters between your thumb and first finger. I have lived on this river all my life, and I know steering pole blisters when I feel them. But if you were a boatman, you would have calluses on your hands, not blisters. From which I deduce that you were steering another man's craft."

"Brilliant." Moktar shook his head in awe. "And how did you know I worked in Timbuktu?"

"I know everyone here in Mopti," said the marabout, "but you I did not know. I could see that you arrived recently because your blisters are still sore. And as for work, your palms are far too soft for a farmer or a builder or a blacksmith. Only marabouts and scholars have palms as soft as yours. And then there is your beard."

"What about my beard?"

"It is unkempt, my friend. It has not been trimmed. From its length, I guessed that you were clean shaven four days ago, and since marabouts are seldom clean shaven, I deduced that you were a scholar. Four days downriver from here there lies a town of scholars and project workers, a town that attracts the softest hands in all of Mali. That town is Timbuktu."

"Genius. But how did you know that I had killed a man?"

"If the truth be told, that part of the story was not in your hand. It was in your eyes."

"I see. But you knew my name as well."

"It follows from the rest, does it not? A stranger arriving from Timbuktu town, steering another man's craft? A fugitive scholar with guilt in his eyes who needs the advice of a marabout? Of course I knew your name."

"Very impressive," said Moktar Hasim. "Well, that changes everything, of course. *Salam alaykum.*"

"*Alaykum asalam,*" said the marabout, offering his hand.

Moktar did not take the outstretched hand. Instead he reached up and grabbed the old man by the throat. "*Salam schmalam,* Al Haji," he hissed. "How soft do my hands feel now?"

The marabout struggled helplessly in Moktar's grip. "Get off me," he croaked. "We had a deal. Why are you doing this?"

"You tell me," answered Moktar, pressing with his thumbs. "What's a quarter of two million mithqals?"

The old man gargled unintelligibly and his eyes rolled up into his head. Then his body went limp.

"A marabout should never reveal his methods," murmured Moktar, unwinding the old man's long black turban and putting it on his own head. "As long as people fear him, he is safe from harm."

TWENTY-EIGHT

In spite of the late hour, Mopti bus station was alive with comings and goings and squawkings and squabblings and the frantic tying and untying of luggage. Rusty buses juddered and honked and performed three-point turns in impossibly tight spaces. All except for Danny and Omar's bus, whose driver had parked, cut the engine, and wandered off. Weary Bandiagara-bound travelers seized the opportunity to stretch their legs.

Cartwheels were Omar's favorite method of leg stretching, and off he shot, cavorting around the bus station like some demented wind-up toy, much to Danny's embarrassment and the delight of the traveling public. *At least he's back to his old self,* thought Danny. *There's nothing worse than a gloomy traveling companion.*

Elegant peddlers sashayed to and fro in the semidarkness, balancing tasty snacks on tightly braided heads. Danny bought a baguette, two bananas, and a bottle of ginger beer, and with his mouth already watering, he got back on the bus to wait for Omar.

There was a man in Omar's seat. The man's face was covered by a long black turban with a slit just wide enough for his eyes. He wore loose trousers, a checked shirt, and brown leather shoes. A length of cord was partially visible around his neck— some sort of amulet perhaps.

"Excuse me," said Danny, pointing. "That's my friend's seat."

The stranger looked up at Danny and his eyes were cold.

There was a long silence, broken only by Omar clattering back onto the bus. "Never do cartwheels in an African bus station at night," he grumbled as he pushed his way down the aisle. "That forecourt is like the bottom of an iguana cage."

Omar stopped short when he saw the stranger in his seat. He spoke to the man in French and the man replied in a gruff voice. They began to argue, and it was clear that Omar was getting increasingly annoyed. Other passengers craned their necks to watch Wound-up White Boy.

"Hey, Danny!" cried Omar. "This guy's unbelievable! I told him I'd been sitting in that seat the whole journey, and he was like 'Good for you—now it's my turn.' What's his problem? Do you think he's dopey or just obnoxious?"

The bus driver started the engine, honked the horn three times, and performed a tight three-point turn. He pulled out of the bus station and rejoined the main road heading east toward Bandiagara.

Omar bent down toward the turbaned man. "I know a good game," he said in French. "It's called throw-yourself-off-the-moving-bus. I'll explain the rules and you go first."

The stranger replied in a torrent of French. Danny did not understand much but he could tell it was not polite.

"Fine," said Omar. "Keep the stupid seat. Remember to keep breathing in and out, won't you?"

Omar came and plonked himself down on the petrol canister next to Danny, a dark scowl on his face. "I know what I'll do with my share of the gold," he muttered. "I'll hire an assassin for matey over there."

"Careful what you say," whispered Danny. "For all you know, he might understand English."

"Of course he doesn't," said Omar loudly. "Poor bloke was clearly last in line when the brains were being handed out."

On into the night they sped. The dirt road was pitted and scarred from months of rain, making for a very rough ride. The boys swayed and bounced and bumped and jarred and wished they had proper seats.

"So tell me about this place we're going to," said Omar.

Danny switched on his flashlight and began to read aloud from the guidebook *Mali on the Cheap*. "'Bandiagara is the main point of entry to Dogon country,'" he read. "'It is a seemingly ordinary Malian town with a hospital, a post office, a police station, and a mosque. But continue south toward the escarpment and you will be astonished. Arriving at the Dogon cliffs is like stepping into a fairy tale.'"

"Prepare to be astonished," echoed Omar in an exaggerated Hollywood-trailer kind of voice. "Meet the Dogons! Let them blow your tiny mind!"

"Fine," said Danny. "If you're going to be sarcastic, I won't tell you any more." He switched off his flashlight and it was dark once more. A sudden rumble of thunder heralded the arrival of rain.

African rain was unlike the feeble rain back home in London; this rain meant business. It rapped hard on the minibus roof and leaked in around the edges of the windows.

"So what's the plan for tomorrow?" whispered Omar. "I promise not to diss it."

"Bandiagara is at the western end of the cliffs," said Danny. "We can spend the rest of the night there and then make an early start tomorrow morning. The village we need to get to is called Tireli."

"That's the place Akonio Dolo mentioned."

Danny nodded. "It's the starting point," he whispered. "We need to measure the correct distance from Tireli and then start looking for the secret chamber."

"And fight off any knight or Nommo who tries to stop us."

Just as Omar said the word "Nommo," a mighty flash of lightning lit up the whole interior of the bus, and what Danny saw in that split second made his heart skip a beat. The stranger who had stolen Omar's seat was no longer facing forward. He had swiveled around and was leaning right over toward them— his face only a couple of feet away. *Such horrible eyes!*

And then it was dark once more.

That man is poisonous was Danny's first thought. His second thought was even more frightening. *How much of our conversation did he hear?*

When the lightning flashed again, the turbaned stranger was sitting back in his seat facing the driver, an innocent passenger on a Bandiagara bus.

Danny cupped his hand around Omar's ear and spoke to him in the quietest whisper he could manage. "Tell me I imagined that."

"I saw it too," whispered Omar. "Nightmare."

"Those eyes. I can't get them out of my mind."

"Me neither," whispered Omar. "And did you see his turban?"

"What about it?"

"He had loosened it slightly. *To uncover his ears.*"

"Do you think he understood what we were saying?"

"I don't know. But you know how people's eyes look when they're listening to a language they can't understand."

"Kind of blank."

"Exactly. Did those eyes look blank to you?"

Danny shook his head in the darkness. No, the stranger's eyes had not been blank. Evil, yes. Greedy, yes. Fiendishly intelligent, yes. Blank, no.

"Not another word until we reach Bandiagara," said Danny.

It was past midnight when the minibus finally ground to a halt in Bandiagara bus station. Everyone stood up at the same time and started collecting their belongings and pushing toward the door.

In the ensuing chaos Danny put his mouth close to Omar's ear.

"We need to escape from Evil Eyes over there," he whispered. "Get your flashlight ready, strap your backpack on tight, and follow me."

Danny opened the sliding window nearest to him and wriggled out headfirst. He dropped to the ground, rolled lightly, and ran off in a half crouch. Omar followed, grinning maniacally as he ran. It was great to be on the move again after such a long confinement.

The boys sprinted out of the bus station, turned sharp left, vaulted a row of empty market stalls, and turned left again. For the last hour or two of the journey, Danny had been studying the relevant chapters of *Mali on the Cheap,* and he had memorized (among other things) a street plan of Bandiagara. A four-minute run from here would take them to Hotel Kanbary, a boarding house on the outskirts of town. According to the guidebook the guest rooms were located in a central courtyard and consisted of white stone-built domes with thick oak doors. In Danny's paranoid state of mind, Hotel Kanbary sounded like an ideal fortress in which to spend the rest of the night.

The rain had made the air even more humid than usual, and the boys were out of breath when they arrived at the hotel. They found a night guard slumbering outside the front gate.

"Bonsoir, monsieur!" chorused the boys.

The guard woke up and greeted them warmly. He fiddled with a bunch of keys and opened the front door into the reception area, a dimly lit dome decorated with Dogon masks and cacti.

"The hotel is empty tonight," said the guard, speaking English with a strong accent. "You boys can have Room 1. I'll show you where it is."

Danny and Omar followed him out into the central courtyard. "What's that?" asked Danny, pointing at a large tank on the edge of the courtyard.

"Snake," said the guard. "Snakes are very important in Dogon culture."

Danny took a closer look. The tank was made of dark wood and had a thick glass fronting. Sure enough, there was no water inside—just pebbles, wood, and a big fat lazy-looking snake. It was curled up in the corner and looked dead.

Omar trotted up to the tank and began to do a strange wafty dance in front of it. "Check me out!" he cried. "I'm a snake charmer."

"Get away from there!" snapped the guard.

"It can't get out, can it?" Omar suddenly looked scared.

"Of course not. We wouldn't keep it here if it could get out. But when people annoy it, it strikes and cracks the glass. And that annoys *me* because I'm the one who has to try and find new glass."

"What kind of snake is it?" asked Danny.

"Puff adder. It lies around for days without moving a muscle, and you'd think it was too lazy to strike. You'd be wrong, of course. The puff adder is an ambush predator. It's watching you closely, biding its time, and waiting for its chance."

"So what would happen if I put my hand in the tank right now?"

"Nothing, at first. It wouldn't move an inch, although if you were very observant, you might think you saw one of its pupils shift a little, or its breathing rate increase a fraction. And then *kazam!*—the next thing you know, it's got both its fangs in your hand and you're off to the hospital to get your arm amputated."

"Respect."

"Exactly. Feel free to look at it all you like, but in the name of the Nommo don't make it angry. Now, here's your room, I trust you will sleep well in it. Good night."

"Good night."

From the outside, the guest room was just as the guidebook described it. It looked like one half of a golf ball, except for the dark wooden door. There were sixteen separate panels in the door, and each panel was ornately carved with a tortoise, a fox, a human being, or a snake.

"Looks like these Dogon dudes are obsessed with snakes," said Omar.

"That's right," said Danny. "I read in the guidebook that a Dogon chief never washes. Instead he gets visited at night by a magic snake that licks him clean from head to toe."

"Eeuw." Omar curled his lip. "Who'd be a Dogon chief?"

The room was clean and mosquito free. Inside were two beds, a ceiling fan, and a large stone washbasin. Danny and Omar locked the door, staggered to their beds, turned off the lights, and fell fast asleep.

■ ■ ■ ■

I run, you run, he or she runs.

Miss Bassett's back was turned. She was writing verb conjugations on the blackboard in large bubblelike handwriting.

We run, you run, they run.

The classroom was silent except for the scratch of chalk on the blackboard. And then another sound—a quiet rattle. The handle of the classroom door was jiggling up and down.

"Please, miss. Please, miss. Someone's at the door, miss."

Miss Bassett turned to look. Her face contorted into a mask of terror, as white as the chalk in her hand. "Run, children!" she cried. "Run away!"

The children sniggered and began to conjugate. "I run, you run, he runs away," they chanted. "We run, you run, they run away."

Something was slithering in under the door. Something black and yellow. The children chanted louder and louder. "I puff, you puff, he's a puff adder!"

"Danny!" screamed Miss Bassett. "Do something!"

Danny woke up with a start and felt a cold sweat on his forehead. He sat up and fumbled for the light. *What a horrible dream,* he thought. *Seeing that snake last night must have freaked me out more than I realized.*

He switched off the ceiling fan and listened as it slowed to a dull whir. And then he heard it—a quiet hiss from the floor at the foot of the bed.

TWENTY-NINE

Time slowed to a crawl. All Danny's senses were on edge. He tried to think of a plan, but his mind was blank with panic—all he could hear was that deadly hissing at the foot of his bed. *There's a snake in my burrow. There's a snake in my burrow. There's a snake in my burrow.*

A decoy—that was what he needed. He set his phone to VIBRATE, slipped it into a sock, leaned over the side of the bed, and sent it sliding across the floor into the corner of the room. The snake slithered into view—beautiful, slow moving, deadly —approached the phone sock, and sniffed. *Not interested.* It coiled round on itself to look at Danny.

"Omar," whispered Danny. "Omar, wake up!" He threw a flip-flop at Omar's head.

"What the—hello? What was that?"

"Grimps! Ring my phone."

"Why? You're right here."

"Just ring my phone."

Omar scowled and fumbled for his phone. Danny climbed out of bed and felt for the edges of the mattress.

Oh no! Here it comes.

Hissing loudly, the snake darted toward him. The front part of its body was up off the ground, its neck flattened, its tongue extended. It was going to strike.

Danny put his hands up in front of his face—as if that would do any good.

Bzzzz-bzzzzzzzz. Bzzzz-bzzzzzzzz.

The puff adder turned its body in midair and launched itself at the vibrating sock. Danny heaved the mattress off the bed and tipped it against the wall, imprisoning the snake for a few precious moments. He dived for the door and unlocked it.

"Come on, Omar! Run!"

They sprinted out into the courtyard, past the empty snake tank, into the reception area. Dogon masks leered at them from the walls.

"Au secours!" yelled Omar. "Help!"

A man appeared—a white man, the owner of the hotel—and Danny could hardly get the words out quickly enough. "Puff adder. Room 1. Quickly!"

The hotelier grabbed a thin metal pole with a kink in one end —a handling stick—from the wall and set off at a run. Danny sat down hard on the floor, his back to the wall, hugging his knees to his chest. Omar's legs were shaking.

The night guard staggered in through the front door, a trickle of dried blood on his forehead. "He hit me," said the guard.

"Who?"

"I don't know."

"What did he look like?"

"I don't know. He wore a turban."

The owner of the Kanbary—a leathery Swiss man called Monsieur Mazot—captured the snake and returned it to its tank. There were tears in his eyes as he apologized to Danny and Omar for the breach of security and told them they would not be charged a single franc for their stay at the hotel.

The boys returned to their snake-free room. It was still only four o'clock in the morning, but sleep was the last thing on their minds.

"Let's think about this logically," said Danny. "Evil Eyes follows our footprints to the hotel, coshes the night guard, and puts a puff adder under our door. It's a huge risk. Why does he do it?"

"Because he's evil."

"That's not enough."

"He's bonkers."

"Still not enough."

"He heard our conversation last night," said Omar. "He understood our plan to go after the gold and decided to do the same. But because he wanted the gold all to himself, he tried to kill us in the night before we set off."

Danny shook his head. "Good try," he said, "but that doesn't make sense. You see, I've been trying to remember exactly what he overheard on the bus last night. I know I mentioned Tireli, but what I *didn't* mention was the distance from Tireli to the secret chamber."

"Forty-nine ghalva?"

"Exactly. And there's no way our friend from the bus can find the secret chamber without that measurement. So why try to kill the very people who would be able to tell him?"

Omar was doing a handstand against the wall, but the scowl on his face showed that he was deep in thought. "The only explanation," he said slowly, "is that he knows the distance already."

"Right," said Danny. "And knowing that distance means he must have cracked the square. And the only people with copies of the square are us and—"

"Oh no!"

"Moktar Hasim."

As soon as the idea occurred to Danny, he knew it to be true. The man who had taken Omar's seat on the Bandiagara bus was none other than Moktar Hasim, the manuscript mugger! When he overheard the boys talking, he must have realized that he had competition in his quest for the gold, and that had infuriated him. He had tried to get into their room at night, and when he found the door locked, he used the adder instead. *He must be a very desperate man.*

"Game over," said Omar, collapsing in an ungainly heap against the wall. "If it's a head-to-head race between Moktar Hasim and us, we might as well go home now. He's a psycho with a massive head start. He's probably on his way to Tireli as we speak. He'll have measured his forty-nine ghalva before we've even had our breakfast."

Danny got up and started pacing the room, massaging his temples with his fingertips. "There must be a way," he murmured. "There *must* be a way."

"Right back the way we came!" said Omar.

"No," said Danny. "First rule of parkour: Always go forward, never back. You taught me that yourself, Grimps."

Parkour is not just about running and jumping. It's a whole approach to living. When you start to parkour, you begin to see the world differently. You see creative solutions to the problems that you face. And the more you practice, the more solutions you see.

A solution came to Danny. It was a fantastic, heavenly, diamond-studded solution, and he fell for it hook, line, and sinker.

"Grimps!" he said. "We need to measure forty-nine ghalva northeast from Tireli, right?"

"Right."

"We can do it in five minutes flat, without walking a single step."

"How?"

"We fly," said Danny.

"Of *course*," said Omar in that sarcastic drawl of his. "I'll collect feathers in the courtyard and you get some honey from the hotel kitchen."

Danny laughed. "I'm not crazy," he said. "I'm talking about Google Earth."

There was a long silence while Omar processed this idea, and when at last he spoke, there was no longer any trace of sarcasm. "Danny Temple, you're a freaking genius."

"I don't know about that," said Danny, "but I do think it might cancel out Hasim's head start. He'll be pacing out his forty-nine ghalva on foot. We'll be measuring ours by satellite. I know who I'd put money on."

Omar slapped Danny on the back so hard that he almost knocked him over, and then together they rushed over to reception. Monsieur Mazot had not gone back to bed. He was sitting in a wicker armchair, steadying his nerves with a large glass of whiskey.

"Monsieur Mazot," said Omar. "Do you have an internet connection here?"

"We have Wi-Fi," replied the hotelier. "A French telecommunications project visited Mali a couple of months ago and brought broadband internet to Bandiagara. You can even use your laptop in your room if you like."

"We don't have a laptop," said Danny.

"Oh dear." Monsieur Mazot frowned. "I'll tell you what. You can use my office computer for one hour, on condition that you promise not to email anyone about the unfortunate snake incident."

"Of course we won't," said Danny. "Thank you."

Access to the office was through a door behind the reception desk. It was a pokey little room decorated with colorful photos of Dogon dance festivals. Monsieur Mazot switched on the computer and left the boys to their work.

The internet connection was good and fast, and it took Danny only ten minutes to download and install Google Earth. "This is your pilot speaking," he said, clicking on the map of Africa. "Let's fly."

Danny selected West Africa and then Mali. He followed the river from Bamako to Mopti and zoomed in until he spotted Bandiagara.

"See if you can find the hotel," said Omar.

Danny zoomed all the way in on Bandiagara town and toggled to SATELLITE to get an aerial image of the area. On the outskirts of town was a cluster of tiny white circles that had to be Hotel Kanbary.

"Fly down into the courtyard," said Omar. "See if you can spot the reptile tank."

"Get a grip, Grimps," said Danny. "We've got bigger fish to fry." He began to pan south and east, and as he did, a huge dark ridge loomed into view.

"We are now flying over the Bandiagara escarpment," announced Danny. "This enormous wedge of sandstone, towering in the middle of the desert, was forced from the bowels of the earth by a violent prehistoric upheaval. Measuring over two hundred kilometers from end to end, the escarpment has always been ideal terrain for fighting off invaders. It was first inhabited by Toloy cavemen, and then by Tellem pygmies, and now by *the* most remarkable people on the face of the planet—the Dogon!"

"Get on with it," said Omar.

Danny toggled to HYBRID so that the names of the villages were superimposed along the cliff. "Komboli," he read. "Ende, Nombori, Dourou, Tireli—"

"Tireli!" Omar leaped high into the air and did the split, producing a loud tearing sound from the seat of his tracksuit. But he did not seem to care. Two million mithqals could buy a lot of pants.

Danny zoomed in on Tireli as far as he could go. The image was grainy, but he could make out some brownish blobs that looked like huts or granaries. They seemed to be built right on the lower slopes of the cliff.

"We'll measure forty-nine ghalva northeast from Tireli," said Danny. "That's eleven thousand two hundred and ninety meters." He put a red marker in Tireli and then began to fly northeast along the line of the cliff. One kilometer, two, three, four . . .

There was a brisk knock on the door and it opened a crack. "Sorry to interrupt," said Monsieur Mazot, peering in. "Would you like some coffee?"

"No, thank you," said Danny. "We're fine."

The door closed, and Danny continued to fly along the cliff. When he got to 11,290 meters he stopped. "Right *there*," he said, dropping a yellow marker onto the exact spot. The marker lay a little way along the cliff from a village called Neni.

"At last," said Omar. "Now *that's* what I call a treasure map! X marks the spot, just like in *Treasure Island*."

"No wonder Sheikh al-Qadi's men never found the gold," said Danny. "According to the story, they scoured the cliff face all the way from Komokani to Pégué, but look—*the village of Neni is even farther east than Pégué.*"

Danny zoomed in as far as he could go. There was a whitish area at the base of the cliff right next to the yellow marker. "What's that?" asked Danny. "It looks too pale for sand."

"If you ask me," said Omar, "it's a massive pile of bones. The bones of countless travelers who have visited the Dogon cliffs down through the ages and searched in vain for Akonio Dolo's gold."

Danny switched off the computer and stood up. "Thanks, Tintin," he said. "Your contribution has been enlightening as ever."

"Where are you going?"

"I'm going to pack my bag," said Danny. "Neni awaits."

As the boys hurried across the courtyard toward their room, the morning call to prayer blared from the Bandiagara minaret. "Come to prayer, come to prayer!" the muezzin sang. "Come to success, come to success!"—the very same words that had buried Akonio Dolo in his tunnel all those long years ago.

THIRTY

Breakfast at Hotel Kanbary should have been a sumptuous affair. Monsieur Mazot brought the boys a pile of buttered croissants fit for a Dogon prince, but they hardly made a dent in it. They were far too nervous and excited. Danny's feet were tip-tapping on the floor under the table and refused to stay still.

"You're well up for this, aren't you?" said Omar, filling his plastic water bottle with ice-cold water from a jug. "Yesterday you thought it was a wild goose chase."

"That was then," said Danny. "Today it's a wild gold chase. Those mithqals are so close I can smell them. Come on, Grimps, let's go!"

They said goodbye to Monsieur Mazot and marched off down the dirt road toward the rising sun. According to the guidebook, there were mopeds for hire at Bandiagara Motos in the marketplace, but when the boys arrived there, only one was available— a little P50, even rustier and clunkier than Thierry's.

"I'll drive first," said Danny, "and then we'll swap over."

They paid a deposit on the bike and set off east on the road out of town. The road had clearly been paved in some distant past but was now a mass of craters and potholes. They traveled along the top of the cliff, with the vast sandy plain stretching away below them.

Someone had set up an orange A-frame tent next to the Bandiagara exit signpost. The opening unzipped as Danny and Omar rode past and a white stubbly face peered out.

"Excuse me!" shouted a voice. "Hello!"

"Let's stop and see what he wants," said Omar.

"No way," said Danny. "We're not stopping for anyone until we reach Neni."

Omar craned his neck to look back. "He's coming out of the tent. I think he's— Wow! Nice bicycle."

"What did you say?"

"The bicycle—it's one of those carbon fiber jobbies with panniers and pouches everywhere."

A memory stirred in Danny's mind: *My older brother is in West Africa right now. . . . He's cycling . . . he's in Mali. . . . Wouldn't want to be DT right now—hehe.*

"He's taking down his tent," said Omar. "He's rolling it up and stuffing it into the bicycle panniers. How cool is that! You could travel the whole of Africa with that bike."

"He's a knight," said Danny.

"What?"

"You heard. I don't know how he's tracked us down, but he has."

"I told you before," said Omar. "It's a simple matter of mobile phone triangu—"

"Shut up."

Danny twisted the accelerator and the speedometer needle crept up to fifty kilometers an hour, the maximum possible speed for this moped. The surface of the road was still slippery from last night's rain, and Danny had to swerve from side to side in an attempt to avoid potholes. This was not a road on which to be doing thirty kilometers an hour, let alone fifty.

"Let me drive!" shouted Omar. "You're going to kill us both!"

The road wove through intensely green onion fields on both sides. Onions were an important cash crop for the Dogon cliff dwellers, and it looked like these villagers were in the middle of harvest time. Even at this early hour, men and women of all ages were out in the fields, filling their buckets with the newly pulled bulbs. Some waved at Danny and Omar as they clattered past on the moped.

"Where's bicycle boy?" shouted Danny. "Can you see him?"

"Sort of," said Omar. "When the road climbs, I get a glimpse of him, and then we dip down again and I lose sight. Anyway, he's definitely on our trail."

"How far back?"

"A kilometer, maybe. Hey, Danny, I've got an idea. All we have to do is collect some onions from the fields here and spread them over the road at the bottom of the next slope. Bicycle boy comes whizzing down the slope, hits the onions, and goes flying. That'll scupper him!"

"I'm lost for words, Grimps."

"And if that doesn't work, I'll just sit backward on the moped with a whole bucket of onions and pelt him when he gets close."

Danny shook his head. "Dear Grimps, what would I do without you?"

They sped over the crest of a hill so fast that both wheels left the ground, then started down the other side into a river valley. Here the fields were even greener and the harvesting even more joyfully chaotic. At the bottom of the valley, women were soaping clothes and babies in a tumbling stream. Grinning goats tiptoed along the bank. Bare-chested men in floppy hats raised hoes and spades in jovial salute. The road ahead led all the way down into the river and out again the other side.

"Stop!" shouted Omar. "We should carry the moped across the ford."

"Chicken!" said Danny, careering toward the river at full throttle. "Where's your sense of flow?"

They rattled down into the ford and ripped through it, sending a delicious wave of spray flying up on either side.

"Geronimooooooo!" shrieked Danny.

He was celebrating too soon. In midstream the front wheel hit an underwater pothole and the whole moped flipped over. Danny was thrown over the handlebars and landed on his back in the shallow water.

When he opened his eyes, the brightness of the sun made him squint. A faint oniony smell hung in the air.

"Omar!" called Danny. "Are you all right?"

There was blood in the water.

"No!" Danny struggled to his feet and waded toward his friend. Omar had landed on top of the bike and was lying across it face-down. Villagers gathered on the bank in anxious huddles.

Danny threw himself down next to his friend. "Speak to me, Grimps!"

Omar shifted slightly and began to sing softly in French. *"Frère Jacques, frère Jacques,"* he crooned, *"Dormez-vous? Dormez-vous?"*

"Are you all right?" said Danny. "Aren't you hurt?"

Omar turned his head and looked up at him quizzically. "Did we get it?" he said.

"Get what?"

"The gold. Did we get it?"

"Never mind the gold. How are you?"

"All right, I think." Omar freed himself from the moped and struggled to his feet. Blood was running from his nose and splashing into the river in heavy drops.

"Pinch your nose," said Danny. "Are you sure you haven't broken anything?"

"Not broken," said Omar. "Just bashed up. And I burned my leg on the cylinder."

A strong-armed Dogon man waded into the river, picked up the moped, and carried it up onto the bank.

"Gana," said Danny.

The man grinned. *"Seyoma?"*

"Seyo," said Danny. *"Uluma seyo?"*

"*Seyo,* " said the man.

Omar was staring at Danny with huge goggly eyes. "You didn't tell me you spoke Dogon!"

"Dogon is one of the world's great languages," said Danny. "Don't *you* speak any?"

"Of course not. What were you saying?"

"I was thanking him for picking up our bike, and he was asking if we were okay, and I was like 'Fine, thank you, and how are *your* children?' and he was like 'Yeah, they're fine as well.'"

"That's amazing."

"Not really," said Danny. "What's amazing is that only a couple of days ago you said you could drive a tank through the gaps in my general knowledge."

During the long bus journey to Bandiagara, Danny had learned a couple of useful phrases out of the guidebook, and he was glad to have the opportunity to use them at last. He had been looking forward to seeing Omar's reaction. He was not disappointed. "Sorry," Omar said now.

"I forgive you," said Danny, "if you'll forgive me for dumping you in the river."

"Sure."

"Then let's get going before bicycle boy catches up with us."

Omar's nose had stopped bleeding. He got on the moped and pedaled hard until the motor sputtered into life. Clearly its brief dip in the river had not done any permanent damage. Danny got on the back and prayed for an accident-free ride.

"Relax," said Omar, opening up the throttle until they were cruising at fifty kilometers an hour again. "I have one of these things at my parents' place in France, and I've never once crashed it."

Danny looked back. He watched their pursuer get off his bicycle at the ford, carry it carefully across the water, and climb back on. *Come on, bicycle boy, where's your sense of flow?*

Their road still ran parallel to the cliff, but it was now much closer to the edge. There was only one row of onion gardens between the road and a sheer four-hundred-meter drop. Beyond that, the Plain of Gondo-Seno stretched vast and desolate as far as the eye could see.

"Look!" said Omar. "There's a signpost marked Tireli!"

He was right. The signpost pointed out a rough track that led between two trees and disappeared over the side of the cliff. Presumably the path continued all the way down the side of the escarpment to the village of Tireli.

As Danny looked, a metal bucket appeared at the top of the path, and beneath the bucket an old woman. She had deep laughter lines around her eyes, and her graying hair was plaited at the sides. *So the villagers shin up here in the mornings to harvest their onions and then go back down the cliff for dinner! Incredible— a whole tribe of climbers.*

"I wonder if old Evil Eyes is down there right now," said Omar.

"Probably," said Danny. "But don't think about him yet. Just concentrate on getting us to Neni in one piece."

"What about Bicycle Bill?" said Omar. "Has he given up?"

Danny turned to look. "He's hanging in there," he said. "Don't worry, we've only got another eight kilometers to go till Sangha, and that's the biggest village on the whole cliff top. We'll lose Bicycle Bill in Sangha, no sweat."

THIRTY-ONE

Sangha was perched on top of the cliff with a near-infinite view over the Gondo-Seno Plain below. It was almost ten o'clock in the morning when Omar and Danny rode over the crest of a hill and saw the village sprawling beneath them, an array of neat mud-brick houses interspersed with onion patches.

Their approach to the village led across a wide expanse of smooth flat stones near the edge of the cliff. A small group of Dogon women were working here, pounding in rhythm, their pounding sticks rising and falling like enormous wooden pistons, happily smashing a pile of onions to pulp.

"Slow down," said Danny. "Let's ask these women where Neni is."

As soon as the women saw the moped coming toward them across the cliff top, they began to sing their hearts out. The song was led by a tall square-jawed woman and echoed by the others in a loud lilting refrain. The ladies danced around the onion pulp in a circle, pounding as they went, sleeping babies tied to their backs. As the chorus rose to a crescendo, the pestles thudded harder and faster on the stone and the whole cliff seemed to pulse with syncopated onion-smashing ecstasy.

The singing stopped as suddenly as it had begun, and the square-jawed woman left the group. Pounding stick in hand, she marched up to the boys and addressed them in rapid French.

"What's she saying?" asked Danny.

Omar tutted in annoyance. "She's saying we have to give them something for their performance. She says that they have sung us their most beautiful onion-pounding song and we must give them each a thousand francs."

"That's ridiculous," said Danny. "We didn't ask them to sing for us."

Omar tried his best to appease the woman, but it was not working. She furrowed her brow and began to remonstrate with him, brandishing her pestle in theatrical rage.

"Stay away from the end of that stick," whispered Danny. "I think she wants to do to you what she just did to those onions."

"Let's get out of here," said Omar, "before we make the situation worse."

They climbed back on the moped, and Omar pedaled like a wild thing to ignite the engine. The Dogon woman hopped from foot to foot, incensed by the bad manners of these two young tourists. But the intended escape was not to be. The motor of the little P50 wheezed and sputtered and refused to start. Omar unscrewed the fuel cap and peered inside.

"What's the problem?" asked Danny.

"Gas," said Omar. "Or rather, lack of it."

"Oh no." Danny looked back up the road and saw a fast-traveling dot fly over the brow of the hill. "Don't look now," he said, "but the knight with the bike is about to join the party."

"Let's go," said Omar. "From this point on it's PKO. Parkour Only."

"We can't just abandon the hire bike!"

"These nice Dogon ladies will keep an eye on it for us if you give them what they were asking for."

Danny was running short of cash, but it seemed he had no choice. He fumbled in his wallet and pulled out a five-thousand-franc note. The queen of the onion crushers grabbed the money and curtseyed in exaggerated gratitude.

Omar returned the gesture with a flamboyant bow. *"Au revoir!"* he cried. "We'll be back for the bike!"

With that, he and Danny turned and ran away across the cliff top toward the village of Sangha, the slap of their flip-flops on the sandstone joining with the deeper thuds of the onion pounders. The wind whipped across the plateau, intensely refreshing and exhilarating.

"Good to be rid of that rust bucket of a moped," said Omar. "It was cramping our style."

"Even better to be rid of the Mashing Matron," said Danny.

"What does she think she's doing? Preparing lunch or busking?"

"A bit of both. You can't blame them for wanting to make a quick buck off the tourists, though. I wonder if they'll waylay bicycle boy."

As if in answer to Omar's question, the singing started up again behind them, as melodious and compelling as any siren song. But the pedaling pursuer was not to be ensnared. He whizzed past the Dogon women without even a *Bonjour*.

"He's catching up," panted Danny.

The village of Sangha looked close, but it had looked close for a while now. The plateau was so flat and featureless that the view across it was dramatically foreshortened and everything was farther away than it appeared—a cruel optical illusion.

"If we can get to the first of those huts, we'll be home and dry," said Omar. "Look at it—it's parkour perfect."

The Dogon huts offered access to their large flat roofs via traditional ladders—deeply notched tree trunks leaning at forty-five degrees. The gaps between the houses were just the right distance for cat passes. The ground was sandy and perfect for *roulades*. Omar was right—Sangha was like a huge parkour playground.

"Look at that," said Omar. "There are moped tracks all over the place. I wonder if we'll be able to buy gas here."

Bicycle Bill was right behind them now, and Danny could hear the wind whistling through the spokes in his front wheel. It was hard to feel frightened of this English knight after their terrifying encounters with Moktar Hasim and the puff adder.

Nevertheless his presence was an inconvenience, like a wasp on a long car journey. There would be no treasure hunting today unless they could make Bicycle Bill buzz off.

At last, the end of the endless plateau! Danny and Omar ran up a tree ladder onto the roof of a house and stopped to catch their breath and plan their next move. The cyclist skidded to a melodramatic halt at the foot of the ladder and glared up at them. His nose was badly sunburned from weeks of cycling in the hot sun. It was hard to take him seriously with a nose that red.

"My name is Vernon Potts," called the cyclist. "Come down from there. We need to talk."

Danny and Omar did not reply. They stood still and gazed out over the rooftops of Sangha. *Open your mind to parkour vision. . . .*

"I know who you are," shouted Vernon Potts. "You are Danny Temple, aged sixteen, freelance programmer and hacker. Your parents live in Australia. Your friend there is Omar Dupont, also aged sixteen, sixth-form student at Battersea Secondary School. His parents live in France. I know everything about you both *and I know what you're up to now.*"

Omar raised his eyes to the horizon. "Neni's the next village along the cliff from here, isn't it?" he whispered to Danny.

"That's right."

"Do you see that chunky baobab tree on the horizon?"

"Right by the cliff edge?"

"That's the one," whispered Omar. "We'll make that our rendezvous point."

"You're traitors to the cause," shouted the cyclist. "You would never even have heard of Akonio Dolo were it not for the knights! You took valuable information supplied by KOAD and then tried to cut us out of the loop. You're no better than common thieves."

Omar took his running shoes out of his backpack and put them on.

"Take your own path through the village," he whispered to Danny. "Think narrow gaps and walls—make it hard for the bicycle to follow. We'll meet at the tree in half an hour."

"Don't ignore me, Temple!" cried Vernon Potts. "I'm fed up with you ignoring me. I tried to friend you on Facebook and you ignored me. I greeted you on the way out of Bandiagara and you ignored me. Keep on ignoring me and I'll disembowel you with a camping spoon."

Danny cocked his head on one side as if listening to a very faint faraway sound.

"Right, that's it!" Vernon Potts jumped off his bike and dashed up the tree ladder onto the roof.

Danny and Omar jumped off and rolled on the sand below. They ran around the corner of the next house, vaulted a mud-brick wall, and disappeared from view.

Vernon Potts looked down. The ground was at least two and a half meters away—quite far enough to break an ankle if you didn't know what you were doing. He climbed gingerly down the tree ladder and got back on his bike but did not give chase. He had spent enough time reading KOAD message boards to know how slippery those two lads were. If they could escape from eighty knights in the confines of Clapham Junction, they could easily evade one knight in this mud-brick maze of a village. He would not give them the satisfaction.

Instead he cycled back over the plateau toward where the rental moped had been abandoned. The women had stopped their pounding and were now rolling their onion pulp into small balls and lining them up to dry in the sun.

Vernon's first impulse was to push the boys' moped over the side of the cliff and watch it shatter into a million tiny pieces on the rocks four hundred meters below. Satisfying though that would be, however, he soon decided that such an action was beneath him. That moped was the property of Bandiagara Motos, and his quarrel was not with them.

He pedaled right up to the edge of the cliff and looked back toward the village of Sangha. It was a remarkable sight. The villagers' huts spilled over onto the steep upper slopes of the cliff, perilously close to the precipice. Vernon planted his feet wide, psyching himself up for a rush of vertigo, then let his gaze meander down the cliff face to the caves. The sandstone here looked as if some gigantic shotgun had peppered it with holes. Amazing to think that the holes had in fact been dug by human hands, each one a comfy Stone Age apartment with a breathtaking view over the plains! No one lived in the caves now, of course, except for roosting pigeons.

Another hundred meters down the cliff face were two rows of miniature mud-brick houses wedged into long horizontal crevices. These were Tellem houses, now used by Dogon people as shrines and hiding places. And perched precariously on a steep incline at the base of the cliff was a jumble of tiny huts and granaries straight out of the pages of a fairy tale. Some of the granaries had tall cone-shaped roofs of thatched grass. Some teetered on wooden stilts and looked as though they might uproot themselves and stalk off at any moment.

I'll take my bicycle down there, thought Vernon. *I'll go way out onto the Gondo-Seno Plain and spy on the escarpment through binoculars. If Temple and his friend appear on the cliff face anywhere within five kilometers of here, I'll spot them. And when I do, I swear I'll make it impossible for them to ignore me again.*

·

THIRTY-TWO

Danny took a roundabout route through the village of Sangha, vaulting, cat passing, and wall hopping to his heart's content. The village was very quiet, presumably due to the ongoing onion harvest, and he made it to the rendezvous point unchallenged and injury free. Omar was already there, and he had that unmistakable post-parkour smirk all over his face.

"Kill me now," said Danny, sitting down in the shade of the baobab tree. "That was the sickest jam in the history of the world."

"Amazing," agreed Omar. "We have got to come back here with the Kinetix sometime!"

"Definitely."

"And look what I've got." Omar took his water bottle out of his backpack. "I was right about fuel being sold here. I passed this wrinkly old Dogon selling it in liter bottles, and he used a funnel to pour it into my bottle. Should be enough to get us back to Bandiagara!"

"Nice one."

"Did you see Potts's face? We left him stranded on that roof like a gnat on a glue stick!"

"We're invincible, bro. We're the Princes of Parkour!"

"The Esquires of Escape!"

"The Connoisseurs of Kong!"

"The Flugelbinders of Flow!"

"The Llamas of Lache!"

"The Runcible Spoons of Running!"

"The Ninnies of Neni!"

"Speak for yourself!"

They leaned back against the trunk of the baobab tree, crying with laughter.

"Salam alaykum."

Danny jumped to his feet and wiped his eyes, cursing himself for having let down his guard so completely.

"Alaykum asalam," replied Omar.

It was a group of Dogon boys. There were five of them, naked from the waist up, and they looked like a rough lot. Two of them carried buckets and trowels. Two had long coils of rope slung over their shoulders. The last one carried a machete in one hand and a walking stick in the other. His left leg was missing below the knee.

"Seyoma?" said Danny.

"Seyo." It was the one-legged boy who replied.

"Uluma seyo," said Danny.

The boys sniggered and dug each other in the ribs.

"What did you say?" hissed Omar.

"I said good morning," said Danny, "and then asked them how their children are."

"Why?"

"Those are the only phrases I know."

"You said you were fluent in Dogon."

"I did not," said Danny. "I just said it's one of the world's great languages."

"Which it isn't."

"Is."

"Isn't."

The Dogon boys looked at each other and shrugged. Then one of the bucket carriers spoke up. *"Parlez-vous français?"* he said.

"Oui," said Omar. *"Comment vous appelez-vous?"*

They began to talk. The Dogon boy translated for his friends everything Omar said, and Omar translated the Dogon's French for Danny.

"They're telling us their names," said Omar. "And this boy here says he saw you jumping off his grandmother's roof. He says it is very disrespectful to jump off an old woman's roof. You should have used the ladder, he says."

"Tell him sorry," said Danny.

"I already did," said Omar. "And now I'm going to ask them what those ropes are for."

"Not for us, I hope," said Danny, with an uneasy attempt at a chuckle.

The Dogon boys began to talk loudly all at once, pointing at the ropes and the buckets and the face of the cliff. Danny could tell from Omar's face that he was intrigued.

"You're not going to believe this," said Omar when the boys finally finished their explanation. "These lads are guano collectors."

"Guano?"

"Pigeon droppings. Their job is to abseil around on the face of the cliff, scraping pigeon droppings off the rock and putting them in buckets."

"Eeuw," said Danny.

"There's nothing eeuw about it, dipstick. It's not like the droppings are still wet. And just think what a buzz it must be. They get to spend all day abseiling and climbing and messing about on the cliff face. Look—I think that lad is going to demonstrate for us."

A slim boy in a baggy green beret was tying the end of the rope around the trunk of the baobab tree and looping a section of it around his own waist. Before Danny knew what was happening, the boy sprinted to the cliff edge and leaped off into thin air.

"No!" cried Danny.

The slack of the rope uncoiled and pulled taut with a loud twang. Danny peered over the edge and saw the boy hanging a few meters down the cliff face. He was standing at right angles to the cliff, holding the rope with one hand and waving his beret in the air with the other. Then he strolled casually up the rock, climbed over the edge, and rejoined his friends.

"Amazing," said Danny. "What is that rope made of?"

"It's made of strands of baobab bark, all twisted together. It's incredibly strong."

"And what do they do with the guano once they've collected a load?"

"They sell it at the market for three thousand francs a sack," said Omar. "Pigeon guano is really good fertilizer, apparently. People spread it on their onion gardens."

"Are we still on earth, Grimps? I feel like I've been beamed up onto some alien planet."

"Meet the Dogons," boomed Omar in his Hollywood voice. "Let them fry your tiny brain."

"I'm glad we came," said Danny. "Even if we don't find the you-know-what, I'm still glad we came."

The boy in the beret stepped forward and said something to Omar.

"He wants us to give him some money," said Omar. "He says he risked his life to show you an important Dogon tradition."

"Not this again," said Danny, raking his hand through his hair. "I thought we were making *friends* with them."

"We were," said Omar. "And friends ask each other for things."

"You don't ask me for things," said Danny.

"Only because you haven't got anything I want."

"Oh."

"Tell you what," said Omar. "We'll give the lad a packet of custard creams."

"We will not," snapped Danny. "We've only got one packet left."

"So what? That lad with the machete has only got one leg left, but you don't hear him complaining."

"Okay, okay!" Danny fished in his backpack, took out the last packet of biscuits, and handed it to the boy in the beret.

"*Gana,*" said the boy, which Danny recognized as "Thank you." He opened the packet with one swipe of his friend's machete and handed the biscuits around to his friends.

Danny stepped toward the precipice and looked down. The cliff face stretched away to the northeast, dotted with caves and Dogon villages. He looked again, and his heart leaped. At the foot of the cliff just beyond Neni there was a patch of whitish ground.

"Look down there, Grimps," said Danny. "It's that white stuff we saw on the satellite picture. Ask the guano guys what it is."

Omar translated Danny's question for the French-speaking Dogon boy.

"*Ce sont des os,*" answered the boy.

"I told you so!" cried Omar. "They're bones."

Danny gulped. "Whose bones?"

The Dogon boys all started talking at once, pointing at the cliff face and waving their baobab-bark ropes. Omar asked some more questions and listened patiently to the answers. Danny felt stupid and left out. He had never tried very hard at French when he was at school, and he was beginning to regret it bitterly.

"It's like this," said Omar when the boys finally stopped

talking. "The Dogon don't bury people in the ground. They lay them to rest *inside the cliff*. You see that cave in the cliff face directly above the bones? From the outside it looks like all the other caves in the escarpment, but on the inside you would find the entrance to a Dogon burial chamber—a natural fissure that goes way down inside the cliff face. Let's say you're a Dogon and you drop dead from eating too many onions. I come along and I wash your body, roll you up in cloths and mats, and then haul you up to the burial cave using ropes and pulleys. Live on the cliff, die on the cliff, decompose inside the cliff, that's the idea."

"Have any of these boys ever been inside the burial chamber?" asked Danny.

"They don't go near it," said Omar, "not even to collect pigeon droppings. Those bones at the bottom of the cliff signal to everyone that the area is taboo."

"So who puts the bodies in the fissure?"

"When a funeral is taking place, two villagers from Neni climb up to the mouth of the cave, receive the body, and drop it down into the fissure. But they never go down themselves. All the ancestors are there, and ancestors must be left in peace."

Danny put his hand to his mouth in an effort to hide his excitement. The more he heard, the more certain he was that the burial fissure was the way to Akonio Dolo's secret hiding place. It was too much of a coincidence—a cave that no one ever entered, situated precisely forty-nine ghalva northeast of Tireli. *Good old Akonio Dolo. How typical that the most impious student in Timbuktu should choose a taboo burial chamber to hide his gold! Irreverent, sure, but intelligent as well.*

The Dogon boys had surrounded Omar and seemed to be hassling him about something.

"What's up?" asked Danny.

"They want a thousand francs each," said Omar. "They say they have told us some top-secret Dogon customs, and we should pay them properly."

"Tell them to take a running jump off the cliff."

"Yeah, right," said Omar. "That's what they do all day, remember?"

Danny looked at the Dogon boys and back at the cliff face. An idea occurred to him. It was a bold idea, reckless even, but he could not get it out of his mind.

"Tell them we'll give them five thousand francs," said Danny, "if they give us their ropes."

Omar stared at him and a look of horror spread across his face. "You're not thinking . . . ?"

"Why not?"

"Now it's official," said Omar. "You're even more bonkers than old Evil Eyes back there."

"Just tell them."

Omar raised his palms as if in surrender and began to explain the deal to the French-speaking Dogon boy. It was clearly a good offer, because the lad did not even consult the others. He grabbed the ropes from the two rope carriers, handed them to

Danny, and took the five-thousand-franc note. Then he turned and swaggered off along the cliff face toward Sangha, followed by his friends. They did not even say goodbye.

"Tourism is ruining those lads," said Danny as he watched them disappear into the village.

"It's certainly ruining you," said Omar. "That was your last five thousand, wasn't it?"

Danny waved the baobab-bark ropes and grinned. "Don't worry, Nommo-breath. Where there's rope, there's hope! It's time to make good our losses with one ginormous win!"

THIRTY-THREE

The boys headed northeast along the cliff top, walking in solemn silence past the village of Neni below. They stopped directly above the burial chamber, and Omar tied one end of a rope around a rocky outcrop.

"Sheer class," he said, admiring his knots. "You'll be fine on that."

Danny swallowed hard. "Are you saying you want me to go first?"

"Of course," said Omar. "" 'Tis you must go and I must bide.' This was your idea, wasn't it?"

Danny took off his flip-flops and put them in his backpack, then fastened the straps so that the backpack was tight against his back. *I'm a lunatic,* he thought. *I'm about to walk over a cliff.* From what he could recall, the guano boy had simply looped some slack around his waist and jumped off. No carabiner, no harness, no nothing. His arms must have been taking most of the weight. The more Danny thought about it, the queasier he felt.

He shuffled backward toward the precipice, hoping that Omar could not see his legs trembling. Cat balancing on a strong metal beam was one thing. Abseiling four hundred meters on a rope made of twisted tree bark—that was quite another. Yet here he was, going through with it. He was already standing right on the edge of the cliff top with nothing but thin air beneath his heels.

"See that ledge down there?" asked Omar, pointing. "If you can reach that, you'll be close to the burial chamber. We might not even need the second rope." Omar went on talking, but his voice sounded as if it was coming from a long way away. Much more audible to Danny was the sound of his own blood pumping in his ears. *Come on*, he told himself. *Get in the zone.*

Saharan monkey. Traceur extraordinaire. *Master of all I survey. I stand alone on the roof of an alien world, and below me stretches a quarter-mile sandstone drop. The village of Neni down to the west, Gondo-Seno away to the south. How many times have I descended from on high and in how many different ways? How many nights has my dream self skittered down a sheer façade using only wits and fingernails? How many mornings have I looked down from a window and felt the dizzy thrill of vertigo and freedom? I'm alive, at least for the moment, and I'm coming down to play!*

Danny stepped down onto the cliff face and let out the rope until he was horizontal.

"Look at *you*," said Omar, peering down at him. "You're a natural."

But Danny did not feel like a natural. He felt tense and awkward, petrified in fact, and no amount of *Master of all I survey* psychobabble was going to make him move an inch.

In the end the heat of the rock beneath his bare feet forced Danny to start moving. The sun had been beating against that sandstone face all morning, and it felt like standing on a radiator. Danny gritted his teeth and let out a snort of mingled fear and determination. Then he moved his right hand lower on the rope and took a step backward down the cliff.

He took another step, and then another. Was it the fear or the heat that was making his palms sweat so much? They kept slipping on the rope, sending jolts of panic through his body like little electric shocks. This was more frightening than the Brunei Gallery descent. Worse even than Battersea Power Station. *Four hundred flipping meters.*

Omar was shaking a fist in encouragement and started crooning that awful Danny boy song, changing the words as he went along.

> "Oh Danny boy, the gold, the gold is calling,
>   From cave to cave and down the mountain side.
>   Hold tight the rope and do not think of falling,
>   'Tis you, 'tis you must go and I must bide."

The combination of fear and adrenaline was too much for Danny. "I'm going to throw up!" he shouted, then turned his head and began to retch. The sight of the ground a quarter of a mile away made his stomach churn even more.

"Do you need me to come and get you?" shouted Omar. "I'll come and get you if you need me."

I'll come and get you if you need me. Gatwick Airport. Bright lights. The Melissa virus in a miniskirt, and Danny's dad in Bermuda shorts. *I can't force you to change your mind, Danny, but remember, I'll come and get you if you need me.*

"I can look after myself," whispered Danny. He took a deep breath and planted his feet wide apart on the rock, then started to walk backward down the cliff face. *Focus,* he told himself. *Get back in the zone.*

Danny was used to doing chin-ups and muscle-ups in training but had never exerted such constant stress on his body as he was now doing. His calf muscles, forearms, and lower back were burning, and he knew it was only a matter of time before he began to cramp.

He pushed off hard with his feet and swung away from the rock face, adjusting his grip on the rope in midair so that he would land a little lower down the cliff. Once he found his rhythm, this proved a much more efficient way to descend. It was more fluid and more in keeping with the spirit of parkour.

Omar seemed to agree. "That's perfect!" he cried. "Flow along your course!"

Down the cliff Danny bounced, hand under hand. When he reached the end of the rope, he let go and dropped the remaining two or three meters onto the rocky ledge below, bending his knees to lessen the impact of the dismount.

"You did it!" cried Omar. "You're the man!"

Danny took his phone out of his backpack and texted Omar. DONT SHOUT, he wrote. TEXT ONLY. CHUCK ME THE SECOND ROPE.

Danny caught the rope as it came slithering down. He climbed up, knotted the second rope to the end of the first one, and dropped back down to the ledge. By lying on his stomach and peering over the rim at the cliff face beneath, he could see the mouth of the burial chamber underneath the overhang, but he knew that if he climbed down the rope now, he would be dangling way out of reach.

A text came in from Omar, two words that made Danny's heart sink. LETTERBOX IT.

The letterbox, otherwise known as an underbar, was one of the hardest moves in parkour, and Danny avoided it wherever possible. It involved swinging feet first through a narrow gap, and if you bailed it at speed, you risked a bruised tailbone or a broken jaw. But Omar was right, of course. In this situation, a letterbox was the right move.

Danny threw his second rope over the ledge, and it tumbled down the cliff face, uncoiling in the air like a lasso. He measured off three meters of slack and held it tightly in both hands, rehearsing the move in his mind. He took a short run-up and launched himself out into thin air.

Three meters out the rope snapped taut, and Danny began to swing back in toward the rock face. *Go in feet first. Keep your body straight. Aim for dead center.* He slid in through the narrow gap, let go of the rope, and lay there on the cool sandstone floor of the cave, happy to be alive.

A text came through from Omar. DID YOU MAKE IT?

YES, Danny texted back. He dug his flashlight out of his backpack and shone it around. The smooth rock walls were daubed with pictures of snakes and men.

The cave was much bigger than it looked from the outside. Moving farther back, Danny came to a yawning hole, about the size of his skylight at home. He could not see the bottom of the hole, not even when he shone the flashlight down it. *So this is the famous fissure down which the men of Neni drop their dead.* He shivered.

Danny clamped the flashlight with his teeth and lowered himself into the hole. He placed one foot on each side of the fissure and started to climb down, assailed by an unexpected pang of guilt as he remembered what the guano boys had said. *All the ancestors are there, and ancestors must be left in peace.*

The rough sandstone provided a good grip for bare feet, so Danny's descent was mercifully quick. As the bottom of the fissure came into range of his flashlight's beam, Danny noticed the blue and white checked patterns of countless rolled-up mats.

The fissure gradually widened into a cavern, and it became clear that the mats Danny had glimpsed from above were just the tip of a vast higgledy-piggledy pile of Dogon dead, spilling down on either side into a spacious trench. Danny stepped down gingerly onto the pile and shone his light around. *How many people are buried here,* he wondered. *Five hundred? A thousand?*

IM IN THE BURIAL CHAMBER, he texted. GOING TO LOOK FOR THE GOLD.

Of course, the signal could not penetrate this far inside the cave. *You're on your own now, Temple,* Danny told himself. *Stay calm. Stay logical. Don't flip out.* He made his way down the mound of bodies and into the trench. Some of the mats were in good condition, their patterns faded but intact. Others had split or rotted away completely to reveal their ancient cargo of dry bones. Trodden on for the first time in seven hundred long years, the bones clattered and grated underfoot.

As Danny picked his way over the mass grave, he raked the walls and ceiling with the beam of his flashlight. "Come on, Akonio," he murmured. "Where did you hide your gold?" This cavern looked entirely self-enclosed. There were no secret cavities, no hidden passages, no glinting alcoves or gold-encrusted archways. Just swathes of checked mats and Dogon dead.

Wait! What was that? Danny stepped back a pace and shone his light at the wall of the cavern. Some kind of graffiti had been scratched on it. No, not graffiti, but a picture, a childlike doodle carved deep into the sandstone by a sharp stone or knife. Danny gasped as he recognized the sketch from the al-Kabari manuscript—a goggle-eyed fish standing on two little legs. *It was a Nommo.*

He hurried forward and ran his hands over the Nommo, half expecting a secret panel in the rock to swing back and reveal Akonio Dolo's hoard of stolen gold. But nothing happened. Perhaps it was just a bit of random graffiti after all. *Unless . . .*

Danny bent down and began to drag the rolled-up mats away

from the rock face underneath the Nommo. After all, the pile of bodies was a lot deeper now than in Akonio Dolo's day—there were seven centuries of extra Dogon dead to be accounted for. Before he knew it, Danny was on his hands and knees, burrowing down into the mass grave. The deeper he got, the more horrifying the task. At this level all the mats had rotted to shreds and released their grisly contents. Danny found himself elbow deep in thigh bones, ribs, and grinning skulls.

"I'm sorry, I'm sorry," he whispered as he cast the bones aside to left and right, but no amount of apology could silence the clamor of accusation in his head. *Have you no shame? You're disturbing the dead! Was this what you came to Africa to do? When did you go bad, Temple? Was it when you hacked Timbuktu to steal the manuscript? Or when you hacked Air France to steal air miles? Or when you hacked this sacred place to steal treasure? You're worse than a black-hat now, Temple. You're a grave robber!*

As Danny worked, he felt himself engulfed by waves of remorse and guilt. But when the upper rim of a tunnel came suddenly into view, the voices of reproach were drowned by a massive rush of adrenaline. It was the same rush he got when he got through a firewall—the indescribable ecstasy of having penetrated the impenetrable. *My name is Pergamon 256, king of treasure hunters: Look on my works, ye Mighty, and despair!*

It took only a few moments to excavate the opening to the secret passage and wriggle in headfirst. The tunnel was a tight squeeze, but it emerged almost immediately into a large drafty chamber. Lying on his stomach, Danny shone his flashlight ahead.

In the center of the chamber, stacked in a single glistening pillar, were two million mithqals of gold bars.

THIRTY-FOUR

Far out on the Gondo-Seno Plain, Vernon Potts was crouching behind a rock with his binoculars trained on the Bandiagara escarpment. He watched Danny Temple make his painstaking descent of the cliff and disappear into the mouth of one of the Toloy caves. *So the gold is in that cave, is it? That's all I need to know.*

Vernon Potts pedaled to the escarpment as fast as he could and leaned his bike against the rock face. He picked up a handful of dust, clapped it between his hands to give them extra grip, and raised his eyes to scrutinize the cliff.

He had done some climbing back home in his native Derbyshire, and this ascent did not look hard by comparison. The weathered face had been pitted and scarred by seven hundred rainy seasons and offered plenty of hand- and footholds. If he could manage the first hundred meters on his own, he could climb the next fifty on Temple's rope.

He started his ascent of the lower slopes, zigzagging barefoot up the rocks like a Nepalese mountain goat. He could hardly believe this was happening. More than three thousand determined treasure hunters had joined the Knights of Akonio Dolo, and where were they now? At home, that was where they were, emailing each other about what might have been. But he, Vernon Christopher Potts, was keeping the dream alive. Upon his shoulders weighed the hopes of three thousand knights, and he did not intend to let them down. He would walk right into that cave and demand what was rightfully theirs—one million mithqals, a fifty percent share of the treasure. It was only fair.

"*Salam alaykum!*" called a gruff voice.

Vernon Potts looked down. A Dogon man was passing the base of the cliff with his donkey cart and had stopped in surprise to watch the white man climb.

"*Alaykum asalam!*" replied Potts.

"Nice day for a climb," said the stranger.

Potts stared. *A Dogon who speaks fluent English—that's unusual.*

"Climbing is like cholera," called the man. "It is highly contagious. When you see another man climbing, every bone in your body longs to get up there and join him!"

Potts laughed. "You would say that. Climbing is in your blood."

"I'm not Dogon, if that's what you think." The stranger left his donkey cart and walked toward the cliff, pulling tight the folds of his turban.

"Sorry. I just assumed—"

"I used to have a Dogon colleague," said the man, "but we didn't get along."

Vernon Potts frowned. There was something peculiar about the turbaned man, a coldness in his voice and manner. The man was coming up the lower slopes of the cliff toward him, jumping from rock to rock with remarkable speed and agility. Vernon Potts turned his face to the cliff and started on the vertical part of the ascent.

"I have a theory about different kinds of climbers," called the voice below him. "Category one: those who climb for pleasure. Category two: those who climb to get to their onion gardens. Category three: those who climb to escape from danger. Which category of climbers do you belong to?"

"I climb for pleasure," said Potts.

"Pleasure." The man repeated the word several times, rolling it around his tongue. "How pleasant."

Potts did not like the stranger's mocking tone. *Who is this man, and why is he following me?*

"Have you heard of the Tellem?" asked the stranger.

Potts did not reply. He was well up the rock face now and needed all his concentration for climbing.

"My colleague Ahmed used to tell me stories about the Tellem," continued the man. "They were little people and they were not very good at fighting, poor things, so they built their houses in cliffside crevices. When Ahmed told me about the Tellem, I put them in category three—those who climb to escape from danger."

So what? thought Vernon Potts. *Why are you telling me this?* His mysterious co-climber was close behind him now, and he seemed perfectly capable of climbing and talking at the same time.

"The Tellem believed that if they built their homes fifty meters off the ground, they would be safe. Ha! How wrong they were. They climbed to escape from danger, but the danger climbed right up after them!" The stranger cackled long and loud.

There was something about that cackle that spurred Vernon Potts to speed up. His movements were imprecise and his breathing was ragged. *What is this odious man trying to say? What does he want with me?*

"Here's another thing Ahmed told me," said the stranger. "Ever since the Tellem disappeared, their huts have been raided for statuettes and bangles. Greedy looters climb the cliff, fill their bags with Tellem trinkets, and then sell them on the black market. When Ahmed told me about those looters, I felt sad and did not know what category to put them in. So I invented category four—those who climb for wrongful gain."

"Go away!" said Potts, dragging himself feverishly up the cliff face. Sweat dripped down his forehead into his eyes.

"Perhaps my categories are too rigid," mused the stranger. "A man who climbs for pleasure might also climb for wrongful gain. And one day he might even find himself climbing to escape from danger."

"Stop following me!" cried Vernon Potts.

"I'm not following you, I'm chasing you," said the turbaned man, and his voice was very close indeed. "Caught you, in fact."

Potts felt a strong hand grab his foot. "Let me go!" he cried.

"I might, I might not," said the stranger. "Whose rope is that up there?"

"It belongs to a boy called Danny Temple," said Potts. "He's in the cave now."

"Which cave?"

"That one there," sobbed Potts, pointing. "Just beneath the overhanging ledge."

"Is he alone?"

"Yes."

"Thank you," said the man. "And now I will let you go."

Potts felt a sharp blow behind his knee, and his supporting leg buckled beneath him. He was off balance, clawing at the cliff face.

"Climbing is like cholera," said Moktar Hasim. "It usually ends up killing you."

Like monkey bread from a baobab tree Potts fell, and like monkey bread he broke open on the rocks below.

THIRTY-FIVE

Danny wriggled out of the treasure chamber, picked his way over the pile of Dogon dead, and was about to climb up into the fissure when he saw the beam of a flashlight above him. Omar must have got tired of waiting.

"Grimps!" called Danny. "I thought you were going to stay up top and keep watch!"

Silence, except for the scuffling sound of hands and feet on sandstone.

If that's Omar, why doesn't he say something? Danny turned and scrambled down over the pile of bones, and his eye fell on a rolled-up mat that lay against the wall of the cavern. *That'll do.*

The body inside the mat was swathed in thick white cloth. Danny pulled it out roughly, rolled himself up in the mat, and lay still, breathing as shallowly as he could.

The phantom caver climbed down out of the fissure and stepped onto the pile of Dogon dead. Danny could not see anything, but he could hear whoever it was moving around. Bones clattered, mats rustled, and then someone spoke.

"*Salam alaykum,*" said a voice, and Danny's heart sank. He recognized that gruff voice from the Bandiagara bus. It was Moktar Hasim!

"I know you're in here, Temple," called Moktar Hasim.

Danny held his breath.

"Isn't gold wonderful?" said Hasim. "It gets its hooks deep into you and turns you inside out. Makes you mad and bad and capable of anything, right, Temple?"

Wrong, thought Danny, but then he began to wonder. Maybe he *had* been changing. He might not have noticed it himself, but Omar certainly had: *You're a traceur, Danny, so stop talking like a happy-slapper. . . . That map has turned you into a real prat. . . . That's a black-hat hack—I thought you didn't do black-hat. . . . We're not criminals, Danny! . . . You're even more bonkers than old Evil Eyes.*

Danny's thoughts were interrupted by an exclamation of cheerful surprise. "Hail to the Nommo, heavenly ancestor!" cried Moktar Hasim. "Monitor, Teacher, Master of the Water." There was a long silence and then a cry of triumph. "*Al Hamdilillalay!* It's still there. After seven hundred years it's still there!"

He's found the gold, thought Danny. *And now he'll find me.*

"I know you're in here, Danny!" called Moktar Hasim. "The young man outside told me!"

Danny's heart pounded faster still. *The young man outside? Omar!*

"If he was lying to me, I'll kill him," said Moktar Hasim. "No wait, I'm forgetting. I already did!"

Danny went suddenly and completely numb. After the numbness, a tightening in the chest and a frightening sound welling up inside. He could not keep it in. A great sob of grief and rage filled the chamber, muffled only slightly by the burial mat.

"So *there* you are," said Moktar Hasim.

The light came closer and closer. Strong hands tore at the mat around Danny's head, pulling away whole sections of the weave until his face was uncovered.

"*Salam alaykum,* " said Moktar Hasim.

The light was shining directly in Danny's eyes, blinding him. He was completely helpless, arms and legs immobilized inside the mat.

"Danny? Is that you?"

This time the speaker was not Moktar Hasim. It was Omar's voice, and it came from the fissure above Danny's head!

Moktar Hasim picked up a large thigh bone and moved behind Danny. "Come down very slowly," he called. "I have your friend."

Omar stepped down out of the fissure onto the top of the pile of mats. He looked at Moktar Hasim and a flash of recognition passed between them.

"Back off," said Moktar Hasim, shining his light in Omar's eyes. "For the sake of your friend here, back off."

Omar backed away with his hands up. "Danny," he said, "are you okay?"

"Yes," said Danny. "Get out, now, while you can."

"I'm staying," said Omar.

"What a beautiful friendship," sneered Moktar. "Now, listen to me, both of you. The gold is *mine,* but if you do exactly what I say, you can still walk away from here. I'm going down to the bottom of the cliff to load up the donkey cart. And you"—he waved his flashlight at Omar—"are going to be my golden retriever. You'll go to and from the treasure chamber with that backpack of yours, and you will throw the gold down to me bar by bar."

"What makes you think I would do that?" said Omar.

"Because your friend is going to stay with me," snapped Moktar Hasim, "and you care about him more than you care about the gold. Am I right?"

Omar glowered. "Yes," he said.

"When I've finished loading up the cart, your friend will go free."

"What if you're lying?"

"Silence!" shouted Moktar, and his voice bounced around the rocky walls of the burial chamber. "Do what I say or I'll finish you both right here and now. Go into the chamber over there"—Moktar pointed with the flashlight—"and start filling up with gold."

Omar picked his way down the pile of bodies toward the tunnel, then stopped and turned. "Please," he said, "at least let my friend have his water bottle. It's hot outside."

"Throw it here."

Omar took the water bottle from his backpack and threw it.

"Thanks," said Hasim, catching the bottle in one hand. "I have a long journey ahead of me. I'll be glad of that."

Omar looked furious. He was about to say something but then seemed to think better of it. He turned away, wriggled through into the gold chamber, and was gone.

Moktar Hasim looked down at Danny. "Does that sound like a plan?" he said.

"Yes."

"Do you think your friend will cooperate?"

"Yes."

"And what about you?"

"I have no choice."

"I wish I could believe you," said Moktar Hasim. "But the plain is a long way down, and I don't want you trying any heroics on the way." He raised the thigh bone high above his head. "See you soon."

The bone came down hard on Danny's skull and he blacked out.

THIRTY-SIX

When Danny woke up, he was lying on the sand at the foot of the cliff. His hands and feet were tied with baobab-bark rope. His head was throbbing, and the skin on his nose and cheeks was badly sunburned.

The donkey cart beside him was loaded with gold. It shone fiercely under the noonday African sun, unutterably beautiful and precious. *And it had so nearly been his.*

Moktar Hasim was staggering toward the cart, cradling four bars of gold in his arms and muttering to himself in French. Narrowing his eyes to slits so that Hasim would not know he had regained consciousness, Danny squinted up at the cliff face. There stood Omar, framed in the mouth of the burial chamber, obediently tossing down the bars of gold one by one. Then he turned and disappeared, presumably to refill his backpack in the once-secret treasure chamber of Akonio Dolo.

Danny craned his neck, but there was no one else in sight. The men and women of Neni were still harvesting their cliff-top gardens, and as for the onion pounders and the guano boys, they were back in Sangha. *Face it,* Danny said to himself, *you're on your own.* The sunburn on his face was painful, and he longed to wriggle over into the shade of Hasim's cart. *I must resist,* he thought. *He doesn't yet know that I've woken up. And right now that's the only thing in my favor.*

While Moktar Hasim strode to and fro collecting the bars of gold, Danny strained against his bonds until his wrists were sore. It was no use. If these baobab-bark cords were strong enough to swing on, they were more than strong enough to immobilize a boy. *If only I had my penknife,* thought Danny, *I could cut myself loose. But it's lying in a Sharp Items bin in Gatwick Airport and I'm lying here with nothing in my pockets except a mobile phone and some biscuit crumbs.*

Not quite. There *was* something else, wasn't there? Thierry had given him a lighter as a gesture of friendship when they had said goodbye in Bamako, and—Danny felt his pocket—yes! It was still there. He allowed himself to feel a flicker of hope. That lighter was his way out of here.

Omar reappeared in the mouth of the burial chamber and began to drop more bars, while Moktar Hasim scurried this way and that at the foot of the cliff, filling his arms with the treasure. There was something absurd about his frenetic gathering of gold.

Bending his wrists this way and that, Danny eventually succeeded in angling the lighter down onto his baobab-bark cords and flicked it on. A wisp of smoke curled upward from the middle of the cord, and then it burst into flame. When Moktar Hasim staggered back to the cart, his back bowed by the weight of gold in his arms, Danny was once again pretending to be unconscious. But he was wide awake, and his hands and feet were free.

The treasure hunter loped off to fetch more gold, and immediately Danny sat up and tore the charred bonds from his wrists and ankles. He was going to make a run for it. He would escape with his life and his enemy would escape with the gold. So be it.

As Danny got to his feet, he noticed a water bottle on the ground near the donkey. It was the water bottle Omar had persuaded Moktar Hasim to take with him—a water bottle that did not contain water. *"I passed this wrinkly old Dogon selling it in liter bottles, and he used a funnel to pour it into my bottle. Should be enough to get us back to Bandiagara!"*

Danny snatched up the bottle and splashed the contents over the cart, dousing the wooden slats and the stacks of gold with a liter of gas. Moktar Hasim sensed the movement behind him and turned just in time to see Danny flick the lighter and hold it to the edge of the cart. *Give me my chariot of fire.*

Ffffup! The blue flame licked all the way across the cart and reared up into an inferno that singed Danny's eyebrows and propelled him backward. Tongues of fire chased one another across the surface of the gold and dripped between the cart slats onto the sand.

The terrified donkey took off at a canter in the direction of

Neni, eyes rolling, flanks heaving, frenzied brays rebounding off the cliff face. Danny took off in the opposite direction, running barefoot over the warm sand. For a moment Moktar Hasim hesitated—unsure of which direction to pursue—but only for a moment. He set off at a sprint behind his blazing gold, screaming at the top of his voice for the frantic animal to stop.

Hearing the cacophony, the Dogon villagers left their onion gardens and hurried to the cliff top, and before long the skyline was speckled with spectators, gazing open-mouthed at the braying blur of gold and gray that careered across the plain below. Some of the young men started down the cliff toward the action, shinning confidently down the rock face using only their bare hands and feet.

When the lashes securing the donkey finally burned through, the entire conflagration rolled to a halt and the crazed animal was free. Unhurt but for a handful of singed tail hairs, the donkey ran at a gallop all the way to its master's house in Neni.

Moktar Hasim leaped and hopped around his treasure. Though the gas on the gold bars had burned away, the wooden cart slats were now blazing steadily. The rubber tires had also caught fire, emitting plumes of black smoke and a stench so acrid that even the villagers on the cliff top wrinkled their noses.

Hasim stood in the donkey's place and grabbed hold of the cart with every intention of lugging it himself. By the time the young men arrived at the foot of the cliff, Hasim was ankle deep in sand and was straining against the fully loaded cart with such wild fervor that he tore a shoulder tendon. Weakened and lop-sided, still he heaved, shaking his head from side to side and screaming like a tormented soul.

When at last Hasim fell silent, one of the young Dogon men spoke up. "That looks like my father's cart," he said to his friends.

THIRTY-SEVEN

New post by **Moira Moran** at **1:40 a.m.**

Manuscript mugger in custody

Not sure if you already saw this on the Afronews website, but Moktar Hasim's been caught! Apparently he was nabbed near the Dogon village of Neni in possession of a stolen donkey cart. He's at Bandi-agara police station right now, being questioned in connection with the murders of Seydou Zan (a Timbuktu boatman), Al Haji Bukari Musa (a Mopti marabout), and Vernon Potts (Ed's brother).

 Here's the thing that interests me: This Neni place is about seven kilometers along the Dogon cliffs from where Akonio Dolo claimed he hid the gold. So maybe it was where he said it was all along. What do u think?

Reply posted by **Ray Phelps** at **3:45 a.m.**

Re: Manuscript mugger in custody

Talk some sense moran or should I say moron? If the gold was where he said it was, how come those seventy-seven imperial guards never found it? And if you ask me, it's Temple and Dupont the police should be questioning. Think about it. Vernon Potts goes to Bandiagara to hunt for Temple and Dupont, and the very next day he gets PUSHED off a CLIFF. Hardly a case for Scotland Yard, is it? The Mali police should FIND those juvenile delinquents and throw them in the TIMBUKTU DUN-GEONS, that's what I say.

Reply posted by **Zwiebel Zwo** at **9:43 a.m.**

Re: Manuscript mugger in custody

The price of gold here in Bamako has plummeted overnight. That can mean only one thing—a large quantity of gold has suddenly come onto the market. Who is selling it, I don't know. Dogon merchants, probably. Whoever it is, our treasure hunt is over.

Don't be too sad, guys. That gold was given by Mansa Musa to the University of Timbuktu, but who dug it out of the ground in the first place? Dogon slaves! So if Dogon people have it now, maybe justice has been done. I just hope they spend it wisely.

Reply posted by **Robin Redvald** at **9:49 a.m.**

Re: Manuscript mugger in custody

No quantity of gold is worth a life. Out of respect for Vernon Potts and the other victims of Moktar Hasim, I call on Ronald Smith, the administrator of KOAD, to close down this group.

Aroba Konaté et Frères Import-Export was situated in a heavily guarded warehouse off Bamako's Avenue de la Liberté. The perimeter fence was topped with barbed wire and patrolled by men and dogs. Danny and Omar approached with trepidation.

"What do you want here?" asked the security guard at the

gate, looking down his nose at the boys. But his attitude changed when he saw what was in Omar's backpack. "Excuse me a moment," he said, then picked up the phone and spoke rapidly in a local tongue. When he put the phone down, the guard was all smiles. "Monsieur Konaté will come down and meet you himself," he said.

Three minutes later Aroba Konaté arrived, wearing a well-pressed suit and an air of quiet authority. He shook hands and led the boys into an air-conditioned office. They looked around at the huge desk, deep leather armchairs, and ornate drinks cabinet, on which stood a cut-glass whiskey decanter and a set of bronze scales and weights.

"I hear you want to sell some gold," said Monsieur Konaté. "Please take a seat."

Omar took the gold bar out of his backpack and handed it to Aroba Konaté, who turned it over and over in his hands, making soft clicking noises deep in his throat.

"This bar was cast during the reign of Mansa Musa," said the merchant. "It is very old—a national treasure, in fact."

"I know," said Omar. "That's what I told my friend here. I told him straight, there's no way Monsieur Konaté will want to buy a priceless national treasure and melt it down and sell it to Europe for wads of—"

"Slow down," said Aroba Konaté. "I didn't say I'm not interested. I just can't export it, that's all. Perhaps I could offer it to the National Museum here in Bamako."

"Brilliant," said Omar. "I didn't think of that."

"I won't pay you more than two hundred U.S. dollars an ounce, you understand."

"We understand," said Danny quickly.

Monsieur Konaté turned around to weigh the gold, and the boys allowed themselves a quiet high-five behind his back. Two hundred dollars an ounce would cover their airfares home, compensate laptop boy, and leave enough change for some very nice souvenirs.

When Danny and Omar left the warehouse, they turned left along the Avenue de la Liberté, heading toward the river and the offices of Air Mali.

"Do you think Konaté will really offer that gold to the museum?" asked Omar.

"No chance," said Danny. "It'll be melting in his furnace before you can say 'priceless national treasure.'"

"I still can't believe the Dogon chief gave us only one bar out of that whole stash. Talk about ungrateful."

"Couldn't care less," said Danny. "For me, it was all about the challenge: find the chamber, get in, look around, get out."

"And I'm a Nommo!" scoffed Omar.

"No, really," said Danny. "The thrill's in gaining access. Freedom of thought, freedom of movement, you know the score. For me it was never about the gold. Not ever."

"Gold schmold, right?"

"You said it, Grimps. Gold is too heavy by far. Weighs you down."

"Cramps your style."

"Lames your lache."

"Stumps your jumps."

"You want to run?"

"Sure."

The boys ran off, heading up the Rue de l'Indépendence as far as the river and then right along the riverbank. *The riverbank path is parkour paradise—along its length are mooring posts, kayaks, pygmy goats, date palms, and watermelon stalls. Open your mind to parkour vision; flow like water over your course. Kong vault, dash vault, tic-tac, kash vault, cat pass, gap jump, dismount, drop. Your will chooses your path, your feeling guides you, your energy propels you.*

"Grimps?"

"What?"

"Do you think there's a parkour scene in Australia?"

"Yeah, sure. Probably. Why do you ask?"

"No reason."

AUTHOR'S NOTE

Often I read a novel and find myself wondering how much of it was true. I don't mean the characters and plot, I mean the setting: the history, the geography, and other bits and pieces of background color. Were they a result of extensive travel and painstaking research, or did the author simply sit down on a wet Saturday afternoon and make it all up? So here's a short guide to *Hacking Timbuktu:* what's real and what's not.

TIMBUKTU

Timbuktu is a real city. It was a great center of culture and learning during West Africa's golden age, the fourteenth, fifteenth, and sixteenth centuries. The Timbuktu Manuscripts Project is also real, and the process of digitizing all those thousands of ancient manuscripts is still going on. You can browse the manuscripts at www.loc.gov/exhibits/mali/mali-exhibit.html. If you stumble upon a treasure map, please let me know. (All website addresses are correct at the time of writing.)

The character of Akonio Dolo and the legend of his amazing gold heist are entirely made up.

DOGON COUNTRY

In 2005 I visited Dogon country in the southeast of Mali. Everything you have read in this book about the cliffs and the Dogon people is factual. Nommo, snakes, burial chambers, onion pounding, guano collecting—none of it is made up. In the words of Omar: "Meet the Dogons. Let them blow your tiny mind!"

Dogon country is an amazing part of the world, but having visited there as a tourist, I do question whether tourism is enhancing Dogon culture or spoiling it.

HACKING

HOPE (Hackers On Planet Earth) is a real series of hacking conferences. It takes place in New York, not in London. Using Skype to "tunnel" into someone's computer is technically possible, as is the "man in the middle" airport hack, but they are both extremely difficult. With cybercrime on the rise, the line between white-hat and black-hat hacking is finer than ever. Try not to cross it.

The snippets of code early on in the book are the programming language C+. My friend Kybernetikos has pointed out to me that my code is full of syntax errors, for which I apologize to other readers who notice them.

PARKOUR

Parkour started in France and has become popular all over the world since the mid-1990s. I first came across it when I watched the *Jump London* documentary back in 2003. I am a big fan of parkour pioneers David Belle and Sébastian Foucan and have spent many happy hours watching their clips on YouTube.

Parkour is now commonplace in action films and commercials, but *Hacking Timbuktu* is perhaps the first-ever parkour novel. I have tried to make the parkour sequences as authentic as possible; they all consist of real moves which you can learn to do yourself. I could not resist writing a few roof scenes, but please note: real traceurs are infuriated by the popular misconception that parkour must take place on roofs.

To find out more about parkour, or to meet up with traceurs in your area, visit www.urbanfreeflow.com. And remember, a traceur knows his or her limits. If you want to avoid injury, start small and build up.

ABOUT THE AUTHOR

Stephen Davies, a missionary, lives in Burkina Faso, West Africa, among Fulani herders. He speaks Fulfulde (the local language) and eats millet. As West Africa director for the charity World Horizons International, he oversees primary schools, craft enterprises, and a community radio initiative. Mr. Davies has written several books for young readers; *Hacking Timbuktu* is the first to be published in the United States. A recipient of the Glen Dimplex Children's Book Award, he also contributes to the *Sunday Times* (London), the *Guardian Weekly*, and *Africa Geographic*.

Mr. Davies and his wife share their home with a horse, five hens, two cats, and their daughter, Liberty Rose. Visit him on his website, www.voiceinthedesert.org.uk.